THE CHRISTMAS MARQUESS

The newly-minted Marquess of Hadlow thought the campaign against Napoleon was risky, but nothing could prepare him for the onslaught of debutantes arriving at his door, with marriage on their minds.

Completely unprepared for this dangerous new mission of finding a well-dowried bride, he trades places with his family's loyal retainer. That way, he'll be able to safely observe the guests from a distance.

It's the perfect plan.

Heiress Bertha Collingwood is on a campaign of her own.

Thrilled to be attending her first house party, she seeks the butler's advice for ways to earn the Marquess's favour.

The trouble is, the butler is so tempting, Bertha's having trouble keeping her eyes on the prize.

CHAPTER 1

DECEMBER, 1820

The team of horses pulled into the carriageway of the Marquess of Hadlow's country estate in southern England.

Dark clouds weighed heavily in the sky. It might snow, or it might keep right on glooming.

Icy wind smacked Bertha Collingwood's cheek as the carriage door opened.

Their driver lowered the steps. He wore so many layers, Bertha struggled to see his face. "You must be freezing from the long drive. Please get warm as soon as you're able."

"Yes, Miss," he said, as a footman from the estate stepped forward and silently offered a hand to assist Bertha down.

Mamma spoke from within the carriage, "Mind your feet, dearest."

"Yes, Mamma." The wind swirled, sending puffs of steam with each word. Bertha trotted towards the shelter of the imposing stone façade of Hadlow Hall.

The wind danced with ice. Bertha tucked her fur collar tighter around her neck.

Mamma, catching up to her, did the same. "This will be the making of our family," Mamma said as they approached the entrance to Hadlow Hall. "A coronet for you, and then my grandchildren shall marry even higher."

Mamma was always getting ahead of herself.

Bertha commented, "We have yet to even meet the marquess. How do we know if he will appeal, much less be marry able?"

"Marriageable, dearest." Mamma made a quiet snort, which sent a plume of steam ahead of her. "Fret not, he will choose you. Of that I'm sure."

"But what about my choosing? Do I get a say in this?"

"Of course, dearest. You get to say, "I do" on the morning of Christmas Eve."

Christmas Eve was only nine days away! What if the marquess was a brute? A hulking, slavering ne'er do well who abused his staff and wife?

Or worse.

What if he were a mimsy fop? A slave to fashion and appearances, wasting money on keeping up with the royal court?

Bertha kept her voice low and said, "Mamma, are you sure you have not squandered Papa's resources on securing that special license?"

Mamma sent a fresh plume of steam into the cold air in frustration. "Of course not. The Marquess of Hadlow wants a wife with plenty of blunt. The Collingwoods desire a title. It's a perfect match. Chin up, my darling. Eyes on the prize."

Bertha's delicate ears burned from Mamma's words. And

the chill. The fur-trimmed hat she wore may have been the very pinnacle of fashion, but it was the nadir of practicality, covering only the crown of her head, leaving the top of her neck open to the elements. Best get inside as soon as possible.

Hadlow Hall's staff hustled into position by the entrance to welcome Bertha and her mother to the estate.

"Thank you for your lovely welcome, now please don't stay out here on our account. Get inside into the warm," Bertha instructed, as if she were the chatelaine and the staff hers to instruct already.

The staff curtseyed but made no such move to get warmer. A butler rushed out the front door to greet them. A far-too-young-looking butler, who had no gloves. Or hat.

Or even a cravat.

In this weather?

His shaven cheeks had the healthy red sheen of fresh apples. His brown eyes glistened with moisture. Possibly the shock of the outdoors too, Bertha reckoned.

Was that a wink delivered in Bertha's direction? Couldn't be, she must have misread the butler's face. In this weather, people blinked rapidly to keep the cold out.

To the butler's confusion, Mamma stretched out a hand to shake his. He was far too polite to ignore her entreaty, so he took it and shook it.

Mamma said, "Please tell your staff to get out of this terrible weather. If they catch a chill they'll be no good to us at all."

The butler spluttered and said, "Capital idea."

To Bertha, he was the perfect specimen for the role, even if he would catch his death of cold if he didn't go inside soon. Handsome in a serviceable way, without being overly distracting. Except that now Bertha looked upon him, he was already proving far too much of a distraction. Tall, with wavy dark-brown hair that curled at the temples in a rather dashing way. Drat. She wasn't here to play with the help. That would really upset Mamma.

Although it would be fun to give Mamma a mild connip-tion, just for a giggle.

The butler rubbed his cold hands together and his neck puckered with goose flesh bumps. He must be very new to butlering. Not that this was a fault. Simply an observation from Bertha that everybody had to start somewhere. Perhaps he'd only recently been pressed into service, what with all the recent changes to the Hadlow line?

The butler dismissed the staff with a directive to "get into the warm," then turned back to address Mamma and Bertha. "Whom shall I announce has arrived?"

What a strange way of speaking, Bertha thought. Her earlier estimate that he was new to the role firmed.

The dark clouds delivered a flurry of sleet. The butler's forehead turned bright pink from the cold, to match his apple-cheeks.

Mamma said, "Please inform the head of Hadlow Hall that Mrs. Stephen Collingwood and Miss Bertha Collingwood are here," Mamma said, giving her very best impression of a grand dame. Then she went and ruined it with, "The *Mar-kee* invited us especially. You may call me Elizabeth."

The butler beamed, indicating he recognized that Bertha and her Mamma were as new to house parties as he was to his position. "This way, if you please," he said.

Elizabeth asked, "What is your name, by the way?"

The second the words were out of Mamma's mouth,

Bertha knew it had to be the wrong thing to ask. Despite studying the rules of society as much as possible ahead of time, the reality of being in situ was nothing like learning from a list of instructions in a guide book. Mamma had even employed a French instructor for Bertha, to teach her the finer points of manners. Alas, some things could only come from being born into the right circles. Bertha, and her parents, were absolutely *not* born in those circles. Not even circle-adjacent. But they did have one thing to their name that created quite the attraction.

The blunt.

"If you are ever in need of my services," The butler said, "You may call me Braddon."

"Thank you, Braddon," Mamma said as they made their way through the main doors. "I do so much prefer using names, even if it isn't your real one. I assume all the butlers here over the years have been Christened Braddon? Formality has a way of distancing people, don't you think?"

Oh dear, Mamma was already exceeding boundaries, mistaking friendliness for familiarity. They were barely inside Hadlow Hall and already their mistakes were mounting.

"When shall we meet the Mar-Key," Mamma asked.

The butler shot her an alarmed glance and coughed. "The *Mar-kwiss* and our hostess, the Dowager Marchioness, will greet all guests at Dinner. Until then, I'm sure you'll find comfort in your rooms."

Satisfaction filled Bertha as she heard the word rooms, plural. One for her, one for Mamma. Lovely.

"I have assigned you and Miss Collingwood a maid each," Braddon made a signal with his hand and two young women stepped forward, seemingly out of nowhere. "This is Brigitte, she will tend to your needs, Mrs. Collingwood. And this is Odette, she shall tend to yours, Miss Collingwood."

Brigitte and Odette probably weren't their real names, but it was the fashion for all ladies' maids to have French-sounding appellations. Brigitte and Odette made a quick curtsey and nodded their heads, ready to serve.

Braddon looked to the maids and said, "You may show the Collingwoods to their rooms."

"Lead on," Mamma said.

Bertha winced.

Odette (or was she Brigitte?) curtseyed again, and said to Braddon, "Yes, my lord."

What an odd way to address a butler? Bertha thought, wondering if they were also new? After all, if the marquess had only recently been found, it made sense the compliment of staff for a house party would be only recently assembled as well.

The fire in the hearth crackled with warmth and there were booklets provided on the shelves for entertainment. Bertha wasted no time cutting the quires of leaves to separate the pages. Making sure nobody was looking, she sniffed the paper. How lovely to be the first to read a new book!

Although Bertha and Mamma would meet the rest of the guests at the evening meal, everybody attending this house party already knew who all the guests were. Many young lads, to make up the male numbers, had been invited. They'd make a convenient second prize for those ladies who did not secure the marquess's favor. Or simply some practise for the ladies before they attended the season proper in London, when it began in the new year.

Bertha did not expect to see much of them, and Mamma probably wouldn't let that happen anyway. Mamma had decided the only man Bertha was allowed to display an interest in was the as-yet unmet marquess. He was the highest-ranking eligible man at the Hadlow Hall party. The next closest was the Baronet of Strathclyde, a place Mamma had declared sounded "far too northern" to warrant developing an affection.

The eligible ladies here ranged from the second daughter of a Viscount, to the granddaughter of a first Earl. Certainly, they were far grander than Bertha, but they too sounded reasonably new to the upper echelons. Perhaps they were just as nervous as Bertha about putting a foot wrong?

Unlike Bertha, they would have had a lifetime of learning the right things to do and say. They would also know that Bertha was not one of them, and never would be.

The guests here would know the Collingwood family ran *The Caller*, the most read news sheet in London. Her elder brothers worked in the family business, and the younger ones were keen to learn the trade when they left the nursery.

Every coffee house in London (and neighboring counties) had copies to read and share with customers.

The previous summer, Bertha had read an edition out loud to a rapturous audience. Alas, that small thrill had been months ago. Once Mamma had discovered the rules (that well-mannered young ladies were not to give speeches in public) her fun had ceased.

Bertha's "performances" were comparable in scandal to dancing on the stage as far as society was concerned.

Hopefully the family's vast fortune might aide a little *societal amnesia* in that regard.

The marquess's family, despite a legacy going back generations, apparently had no fortune remaining at all.

Desperate to find out more information about her soon-to-be-betrothed, Bertha changed out of her travelling clothes into an afternoon gown and went off in search of Braddon the Butler. He must know more about this mysterious marquess.

She'd barely made it down the hall before she saw her target, near the top of the stairs.

"Braddon, just the person I was looking for." Bertha beamed.

Her quarry turned, and his eyebrows rose towards his hairline, creating arches in his forehead.

Bertha continued, "I was rather hoping you could be of assistance."

He tilted his head but said nothing.

She rushed in to fill the silence. "You see, this is my first house party, and I am keen to make an excellent first impression on the marquess." This time she pronounced it Mar-kwis, as he had earlier.

Braddon's mouth quirked, but did not smile. "Of course."

"And, you see," Bertha fidgeted and became flummoxed. She knew the previous marquess had passed sometime in October. And there had been a great search. "We have a great deal in common, if you think about it. I am rather new to society, and for all appearances, the marquess is new to *marquessing*, having only recently been found, as it were, and so that is why in some ways ..." She trailed off, embarrassment overtaking her. With a quick check over her shoulder to make sure they were unobserved, Bertha steadied herself. "I want to make sure

I don't make any mistakes, and I think you're the perfect person to help me."

His eyebrows rose even higher.

"We're both new to this," Bertha rushed on. "You and I. I can tell that you are very new to the position."

Braddon's face relaxed and he let out a sigh. "You can tell?"

"Oh yes, It's quite apparent. But this is a good thing. We may assist one another. A kind word here and there, perhaps if you have the ear of the marquess, you may recommend my charming personality? I feel it incumbent upon myself to alert you to the knowledge that Mamma has already secured a special license."

Braddon's mouth opened and closed, as if he had something to say but it wouldn't come.

Bertha again filled the pause. "In some ways, It's rather refreshing. I'm so new to this, you're so very new to this. Well, almost new. I was already familiar with the family situation. Because of reading The Caller. We ran articles about the search for an heir. It reminded me of the scramble after poor Princess Charlotte passed."

Braddon rubbed his temple. "You're that sure the marquess will propose to you?"

"I'm not at all sure, which is why I request your help. I have yet to meet the man, and I have not a clue what he likes or dislikes. For all we know, he could be a recluse. He hasn't even been to London to be presented to the King."

Braddon swallowed. "That's something I ... did not realize the marquess should do?"

"Oh goodness, please do not misinterpret my meaning. This is not a fault of yours, I can assure you. It's merely if people wish to be able to attend court or ... I guess move in court circles. But perhaps the marquess of Hadlow does not wish to do so, and so that is not a priority. He has barely received his coronet, he can't possibly know all the rules."

"Quite right," Braddon said, and he rewarded Bertha with a smile.

It was a kind smile, that spread warmth through Bertha.

"But as a good butler, I should let the marquess know that this is a step he should take."

"Yes. And you will need to find a good tailor and be able to host more parties here as well. Oh goodness! I wonder if we are in breach of protocol by attending a house party before the season, before the marquess has visited the king?

"Is that something ... to worry about?"

"Perhaps ..." she tried to remember the many, many rules of the society she dearly wished to be accepted into. "Perhaps it is only for ladies to be presented to the king?"

Braddon asked, "Have you been presented?"

"Oh," Bertha blushed. "I beg you please not mention this to the marquess, but I do not believe I will ever receive an audience with King George. Not after the yards and yards of terrible things my family has printed about him in The Caller."

Braddon swallowed.

Bertha pressed on. "But it is of no matter, not really. If not for The Caller, we would not be so very wealthy, and I do believe that's where my attraction to the marquess lies."

Braddon swallowed again and said, "Indeed."

"If anything," Bertha blundered on, "I merely haven't been presented yet. With a large enough donation, I'm sure it will happen. And honestly, if the king weren't such a brazen producer of scandal, there would be nothing to print on that matter."

Braddon laughed out loud and turned it into a cough. "I'm not entirely sure that's how it works. My understanding is that we pay our respects to the king by turning a blind eye to any indiscretions."

"That may have been the case in the past, but the king has made ever so many indiscretions."

Braddon shook his head, "Miss Collingwood, I must ask, with so much already stacked against you, how do you propose to win the marquess's favor?"

"Well..." Bertha fossicked about in her brain for the right answer. For someone so new to socializing, she already had several marks against her. The king despised her family, there was no getting past that. Would being associated with the Collingwoods tarnish a coronet? "Because ... I'm pleasant to look upon, I'm witty and I'm rich."

Braddon nodded his head firmly and said, "Indeed."

Bertha beamed and said, "Exactly. Now if you could see to it that the marquess and I cross paths as often as possible, so that he may learn of my many desirable qualities, that would be an excellent thing."

"And what should I say to the other eligible ladies who request the same of me?"

"You may feel free to ignore them. I am the wealthiest heiress here, and if the staff here want to guarantee their continued employment, their master needs a source of funds."

Braddon winked. "A most desirable quality indeed."

As the evening closed in, the maids dressed Bertha and Mamma for dinner and they made their way to a sitting room near the dining hall. Braddon and several staff were here, offering drinks to the guests as other staff bustled around with tapers to light the remaining beeswax candles in their sconces.

They cast a golden light into the room and delivered such a pleasant aroma.

Worry tickled Bertha's nerves. Every seat in the waiting room had a plump cushion. Warm, thick drapes hugged the windows. The fireplace held a glowing fire, and there seemed no shortage of fuel.

She whispered to Mamma, "I see no evidence of a lack of funds."

"Yes?"

"Our rooms are quite comfortable as well. How can the marquess be incentivized towards marriage if he appears so comfortable? Does he have a mysterious benefactor?"

"He does indeed," Mamma whispered back. "Your father has paid quite the King"s Ransom to make the new marquess amenable to our family, and your charms."

Bertha mouthed, "O" and sipped her wine. Which, given Mamma's recent information, had probably come from her father's own cellar.

Everything had been planned to go Bertha's way. All she need do for the next eight days was to smile and be pleasant, and she and the marquess were as good as married.

Bertha and Mamma were the fourth party to enter the dining hall. There was a slight amount of confusion as the butler struggled to work out where to place the rest of the party.

Oh goodie. Time to meet the Mar-kwis.

The dowager stepped forward. Somebody off to the side, oh, it was the butler, introduced them.

"The Dowager Marchioness Lady Hadlow, Mrs. Stephen Collingwood, and Miss Bertha."

"My lady," Mamma said with a curtsey. Bertha followed her

Mamma's cue. Immediately after the curtsey, she looked about the room. Where was this marquess everyone had come to see?

The Butler continued and waved his hand in the direction of another man. "The marquess of Hadlow, Mrs. Stephen Colling-"

"-Lud!" Bertha gasped. "He's so old!"

Gasps echoed through Bertha's ears. She'd probably made one herself, she couldn't be sure. Others drew breath. Somebody else snorted. Mamma looked set to faint. All that hard work, all those lessons, all that money, and Bertha had gone and ruined everything at their very first meeting.

How desperately Bertha wished to retract those words. Alas, they were out now and everyone had heard them. The old marquess – neck more creased than an unmade bed – made a slight cough into his closed hand. He became so discombobulated he appeared to remove his own chair, until his butler stepped in and did the duty for him. The rest of the staff also pulled chairs out to assist in seating the assembled guests into their positions.

In the ensuing noise of moving furniture and people, Bertha's Mamma warned under her breath, "Hold your tongue."

Well yes, all very excellent advice, but far too late for the shocking way she'd announced herself to the entire house party and the marquess and the dowager ... who probably had the marquess's ear and would no-doubt be recommending Bertha and her Mamma be called home forthwith.

Heat charged up Bertha's neck, no doubt crimsoning her face into the bargain. All this work, all this expense and organizing to get her to a house party hosted by a marquess and she'd gone and insulted him, in front of an audience, at their very first meeting!

The only saving grace, Bertha hoped, was that he might have trouble hearing. Given his advanced age, that might be a possibility. But everyone else had heard her, and those who hadn't would not doubt hear about it later.

Her outburst aside, the rest of the dinner proceeded apace. Staff brought out tray after tray of delicious hot and cold dishes. The guests thanked the marquess and the Dowager marquess - who looked far too young to be his mother - for their fine meal. Bertha kept her thoughts to herself. She only thought the Dowager looked far too young to be the marquess's mother, and did not speak them. The Dowager must have been married to the pervious marquess, and must have been a second or third wife.

It was all too confusing. Taking Mamma's advice, Bertha held her tongue and pushed her thoughts to the very base of her slippers. Fixing on a smile, she consoled herself that it was early days yet. Somebody else was bound to say something silly in the ensuing week. A scandal had to unravel that would put this petit faux pas into the shade.

As the next course arrived, Bertha occasionally glanced towards the head of the table. The old marquess's hand shook as he lifted his soup spoon to his lips. When one of the gentlemen guests made a toast to his good health, he required two hands to lift the glass to his lips.

Perhaps, all things considered, it might not be so bad if the marquess did not find favor in her? This was only her first house party, surely there would be so many more to come?

There were so many attractive, younger men here. Many of the debutantes in attendance were searching for a suitable match - or at least, their mammas were - because they needed to marry well. However, Bertha had no such restrictions. Her father, "The Mushroom," people called him, had amassed a good and rapid fortune with the news sheet and had settled an annuity on Bertha. Whatever happened, whomever she married, she would live comfortably for the rest of her life. Her father had drawn up extensive contracts to make sure the sum stayed with Bertha and did not transfer entirely to her husband upon her marriage. Her father assured her this kind of thing was happening regularly America. Apparently over their former colony, many wealthy families only had daughters, and they were creating their own new laws to suit themselves. Would it really become standard here in England though?

As much as she loved her own company, there were people present and she really should speak with other guests, lest they think her rude or insipid.

She turned to the gentleman on her right and asked, "And what is it you do?"

He froze, spoon held aloft, in complete puzzlement. Then managed a single word. "Do?"

"Yes, "do"? What do you do?" Bertha pushed on. She added a smile, as if to ease his shock that she'd asked him a question.

"Er ..." he put his spoon down. "I do very well, thank you."

He then turned to his right and caught the young lady's attention and started an entirely new conversation.

How odd!

Bertha turned to see the gentleman on her left looking to her.

He said, "I believe you have confused your left and your right."

"That's as may be," Bertha said, "But tell me this, if all seated turn to their right, we should all be looking at the back of our neighbor's head."

He made a nod that conveyed his impression she was not all quite there. "It is the gentlemen who turn, and the ladies who remain still, waiting for us to engage them in conversation."

"Jolly good then. Let's conver-sate," Bertha said. "What do you do?"

Again, her question had the freezing effect on his demeanor. Was there something so terribly wrong in asking? "I merely enquire as to your trade, Mister ... ah? I'm so sorry, I'm terrible with names. It's a personal failing. I'll start. Have you heard of the new laws in Austria, where women may now choose their own profession?"

He seemed struck dumb, and blinked a few times. Then he dabbed his face with his napkin and appeared to gaze at the Hadlow family portraits lining the walls.

Bertha cast her gaze across the room to Mamma, where she made the tiniest of shrugs. Mamma blinked slowly and appeared to breathe out her disappointment.

The butler was here, looking dashing, and appropriately warm this time. There was color in his cheeks, but not from the cold. Bertha noticed he wasn't doing very much in the way of butlering. He appeared to be quietly examining all the eligible ladies present. Ah, perhaps he was compiling a dossier on the ladies, to present to the marquess at a later time? In which case, maybe all was not lost?

Yes, she'd badly blotted her copy book with her outburst. But if she had the butler on her side, the marquess would see that she was a good choice after all?

Her gaze wandered to the marquess, wondering if she'd imagined how very old he appeared.

Alas, his hand trembled as he held the fork towards his mouth.

What a disaster!

She caught her mamma's gaze again and made a slight shake of her head, as if to say, "I tried, but this is hopeless."

Mamma, in turn, gave a stern warning look, as if to say, "You must."

Both Bertha's table neighbors were conversing with other ladies, so she found herself looking at the Butler again.

His eyes alighted on her, sending a warm flurry flurrying somewhere inside her. Bertha smiled and dipped her head a little in acknowledgment.

He winked.

Absolutely no mistaking it this time. The Butler had winked. An impertinent, deliberate, scandalous wink.

Not knowing where to look, heat rose in Bertha's neck. What could all this winking possibly mean? Was she in the clear for the marquess's hand, or was the Butler looking for a romance for himself?

The thought shocked Bertha and the heat from her neck burned across her face.

"My Lord, I cannot see how this farce can continue," the

real Braddon said to the real marquess of Hadlow as he changed the young man into his nightclothes, long after dinner ended. "The young ladies were devouring me with their eyes."

The real marquess gave a soft whistle and patted Braddon's hand away. "I can dress myself."

"Sorry, sir. It's habit. The previous marquess often struggled."

"I bet he did. But I dressed myself in the regiment and I'm not about to stop now. And you, old man, are not about to give the game away, got that? We've started this charade, we may as well finish it."

"Is it fair on the young ladies, Sir?"

"Of course, not, but life isn't fair, is it? If it was, my brother would still be here and I'd be living anonymously on the Continent."

"The staff would be looking for new employers." Braddon suggested.

"If my brother hadn't been so fat headed."

"On the positive side of the leger, sir, we discovered you had not died at Waterloo."

He made a sarcastic, "Huzzah!" and bade the butler good night.

After their maids dressed Bertha and Mamma for bed, they sat for a little while by the fire, reliving the disastrous dinner. "I think the dowager was a second wife to the previous marquess, but they did not have any issue. "Not completely her fault, it does take two. Hence the reason they are very much in need of an heir now for the new marquess. It took long enough to find him, and he's hardly a spring lamb."

"Oh Mamma, I do appreciate everything you and father do for me, but ... I am going to have quite the difficult time of it getting him to compromise me. He doesn't even appear to be able to compromise his own meal."

Mamma let out a hearty laugh, "That tongue of yours will land you in trouble, but you do make me laugh! Now please, only in private. When we're in public, I beseech you to keep your thoughts to yourself."

"I shall not Miss Blount myself, Mamma dear."

"*She sighed not that They stay'd, but that She went*," Mamma recited. "My mother read that often to me, in order to keep me in line, and that is why I read it to you."

"Did it work?" Bertha giggled.

"What do you think, chit?" Mamma said with a wink.

"I think I shall work very hard tomorrow to behave impeccably," Bertha promised. Then she kissed Mamma on the forehead and took herself to bed.

CHAPTER 3

The sun poked through the gap in the blinds, spearing Bertha in the face. Another day closer to Christmas Eve, one less day to win over the marquess.

The sun, however, was welcome. The sleet-filled clouds must have moved on at last. Bertha rose from her bed, placed her slippers on and crept to the window. At this time of year, the sun stayed low to the horizon and packed far less punch than it would in six months" time.

What a view greeted her from the window! Rolling green fields, a lake with mist steaming from it, rambling gardens and so many lovely walks (with hidden nooks, just perfect for the plan.)

Oh dear, it truly was idyllic. Perhaps she *could* go through with this after all.

Alas, the one man she couldn't get out of her head was Braddon the butler. She was supposed to be romancing the marquess, but every time she thought of the wrinkled parchment in men's clothing, her mind wandered to his servant. His winking servant.

"Mamma, perhaps It's best we go home?"

"Nonsense dear. We are here for the duration. It would be a terrible insult to our hosts to leave early."

"I don't think I can do this."

"You'll be fine. You barely spoke to the marquess last night at dinner. I need to you make an effort."

"But that's just the very problem, Mamma. I don't want to *make an effort*. He's older than Papa."

"My darling sweet, that's what makes it all the better. He won't be around for much longer. You can make his twilight years so enjoyable, and then when he goes, you'll have a title and we'll have our connections and can keep connecting your brothers."

"This is really about my brothers, isn't it?"

"Of course not."

"But it is. I'm not even the oldest. Rupert is the oldest, why doesn't he marry the Dowager marquess?"

Mamma clapped her hands. "Oh, what a brilliant idea! I must send a letter and summon him. Oh but, what if the Dowager cannot have children? That would be a terrible waste."

Bertha scowled at her mother's dismissive tone. "I will do my best, Mamma. But I'm afraid this entire house party may be for naught. If only he was younger..."

"He might not be all that old. Perhaps he has been ill? Anyway, we shall talk no more of this. We each have our jobs to do - you need the marquess to compromise you, and I need to witness it. Be ready."

Having a truly beautiful home softened the blow of marrying such a doddery old man. Perhaps he would look a little better in natural light, rather than last night's candles? Yes, it had to be the candlelight casting such harsh shadows over his face, emphasizing every crag and jowl.

Making her way downstairs, Bertha wandered the halls, exploring rooms. One day this estate could be hers, so why not get familiar with the layout?

Noises came from the staff areas below. If she were to be the lady marquess, it would be to her advantage to familiarize herself with the staff, and they with her.

How odd indeed to find the old marquess himself down here amongst the lower classes, counting the silverware.

"Can I help you, Miss Collingwood?" He said, on seeing her there. He didn't seem at all bothered by her appearance. As if it was his regular duty to do these things. How puzzling.

"I didn't know you personally counted the silver?"

"Of course I"- he stopped, mouth open. Then he closed it and made a serene face. "I shall get Braddon to finish this. After all, It's his task."

How very, very puzzling. "Have you had issues with the honesty of your staff, marquess Hadlow?" Oh dear, was that breaking propriety? Bertha rushed on. "Goodness, that's so impertinent of me to ask such a question. I truly do not know the right things to say, much of this is new to me."

"Indeed," he said, confirming her embarrassment.

Heat rose up her neck as she took in his appearance this morning. He did seem slightly younger ... or perhaps that was merely wishful thinking that she look for the best in him? "My Lord," she began again, "I do beg your forgiveness ... I throw myself upon your mercy to please forget my bluntness and inappropriate outburst last eve."

"Certainly," he said, and as Bertha waited, she realized he would say nothing more. "I have created quite the wrong impression, I am usually far better behaved and -"

"Think nothing more of it."

"It's a terrible fault of mine," she ventured. "I am prone to bouts of honesty at the worst of times."

"Goodness." He managed.

Wait. Bertha's mind reeled. He'd forgiven her? At least, that's what she thought had just happened. *Had* that just happened? She'd best check. Far better to make sure, just in case. "I thank you, good sir, for being such a magnanimous host."

He merely nodded, indicating to Bertha that the issue was indeed closed.

It gave her courage to talk more freely. "I do hope we have some outdoor activities today. It will be cold, but the sun is out."

"Indeed. And I hope very much you enjoy them."

"So, we are to venture out of doors? How delightful." Only now did Bertha realize she and the marquess were having a real conversation. It was stilted, he seemed a man of few words. What a pity Mamma wasn't here to witness how much she was trying to *make an effort*.

The marquess then said, "There will be some games in the afternoon, in the gardens."

"Oh, how lovely! I do hope the weather holds for us. Will I

see you at the games as well, or will it only be at dinner? You see, I mean, please forgive me, I don't fully understand what the rules of these house parties are, and so I was rather hoping you'd take me ... under your wing?"

Her Mamma would have been so proud of her making such a *suggestive* suggestion. If only she were here to witness!

He looked at her sweetly, but instead of answering her question, he asked something completely different. "Do you require refreshments? I'll have the staff send them up to your rooms, should you wish it."

"Oh, goodness, that would be lovely. But you needn't bother yourself, I'll find the butler, or someone."

He looked as if he was about to say something and then let it drop. "Good morning to you, then."

They stood there, neither saying anything for a few beats, until Bertha suddenly realized he'd dismissed her. "Oh, goodness, you will have to forgive me again, where are my manners? Thank you, and good morning." She turned to leave, then quickly turned back to add, "My lord."

Keen to enjoy the weak sun, and even more keen to shake her restless spirit, Bertha and Mamma took a turn in the gardens.

"Oh yes, this will suit me very well," Mamma said as she looked about.

"What will?"

"When I come to visit you, and the grandchildren. If the grounds are this pretty in winter, I can only imagine how glorious they will be in summer. I must speak with the

Dowager about her accommodations. She will remain, obviously, but I want some reassurances from her that she will not interfere."

Bertha had to press her teeth together to prevent a scathing comment bursting forth. Mamma of course wasn't interfering at all, no, not in the slightest. She only wanted what was best for her daughter.

The Dowager, Bertha realized, might be feeling apprehensive of *her* situation. "Please reassure the Dowager that should the marquess and I marry, she will always have a home here."

"Until she remarries," Mamma said, then swiftly changed the topic. "This is very clever and forward thinking. See these walled gardens with the fruit trees? The brick walls keep the heat in. Look, many of them still have apples and pears on the branches. How productive! Oh yes, this was definitely a good idea to organize the house party."

It sounded to Bertha's ears as if Mamma had organized *everything*.

Perhaps she had?

They turned the corner to find Braddon the butler in deep discussion with one of the groundskeepers.

"Oh, I'm terribly sorry to interrupt," Bertha said.

"Merely admiring the kitchen gardens," Mamma added.

Braddon gave a broad smile and winked at Bertha.

The outrageous flirtation made something flip in her belly. Impossible!

He had to stop being so dratted familiar with the guests. Sure, Bertha might not know all the rules of staff, but she was confident that flirting with guests who were here to woo their employer was completely out of the question.

Braddon spoke as if he'd done nothing out of the ordinary, "This here is the groundskeeper, Thomas, he is imparting all he knows about growing food for the estate."

A lovely thing to do, for sure, but why would a groundskeeper need to tell a butler about the food? Bertha was still so new to this, and didn't understand who did what in a place like Hadlow Hall. Perhaps now would be a good time to learn. "I too would dearly love to learn all there is about how Hadlow Hall operates."

Mamma joined in, "My darling Bertha here has caught the marquess's eye, and there will be a wed-"

"-Now Mamma, let's not get ahead of ourselves."

A broad grin spread over the butler's face. The groundskeeper looked to the soil by his feet and said nothing. However, from the jerking of his shoulders, he appeared to be filled with mirth.

"Does something amuse you?" Bertha asked.

Braddon cleared his throat into his gloved hand. "Allergies."

At least he was wearing gloves today. They were a soft leather, and looked beautifully made, even at this distance. They must be an old pair of the marquess's.

The groundskeeper made sneezing sounds. "The cold tickles my nose, ma'am."

Just then a brown tabby cat leapt onto the top of the walled garden, its tail flicking. The small birds nearby began raucously squawking out a warning to their friends, the tabby prowled, its teeth chattered in anticipation. The birds flew off to a safer distance.

"Would you like a tour?" The butler asked. "Thomas was

only just now telling me about the varieties that do best at this time of year. We have plentiful apples and pears."

"Aye, and Cat keeps the birds off, don't you Cat?" Thomas held his weathered hand out toward the animal. The cat rubbed its neck into his fingers, then scarpered off.

"I should so much enjoy a tour," Bertha said, then shivered because she'd been standing still for too long.

"Here, take my fur," Mamma said, wrapping the animal skin around Bertha's neck. "We can't have you catching a chill before the marquess has a chance to propose."

The groundskeeper sneezed again.

"What about you, Mamma?" Bertha asked.

"I'll go inside and get another. You learn all you can about the estate, my dear," Mamma said, then retreated to Hadlow Hall.

The Butler made a rueful smile, "I too am learning as much as I may about the estate."

Bertha could not restrain a smile. "So, you *are* new to this?"

Braddon said, "I was not aware I had appeared so blatantly unschooled?"

Oh, he was definitely unschooled, even without the outrageous winks in her direction. Not that Bertha felt able to comment upon it, as even thinking about those winks had a fresh blush gathering under her chin, ready to spread across her face at the slightest provocation. "I meant no offence by the comment. Merely an observation that you may have been only recently appointed as butler to Hadlow Hall."

"Your observation is correct. I hope I have not been too remiss in my duties."

The groundskeeper sneezed again.

"Perhaps you should go indoors my good sir," Bertha

directed her comment to Thomas. "You appear to be catching a chill yourself."

"No, miss, I mean, ma'am. My lady. I'll soon heat up once I get back to work."

"Please take good care and head indoors."

"That is very kind of you," the butler said. "To worry about the health of staff."

"I don't like to see anyone sicken or suffer," Bertha said.

Braddon murmured, "Or are you merely attempting to secure a private audience with my good self?"

That familiar prickly heat threatened to erupt over Bertha's cheeks. "Heavens above!" Perhaps he was testing her resolve, pushing to see if she really was suitable for the marquess, or whether she'd fall at the feet of a handsome man - any handsome man - who paid her a compliment? Straightening her spine, Bertha found a new topic of concern. "Despite the inclement season, the gardens appear productive. I see a wide variety of cabbages here. And the cauliflower is simply abundant."

"Aye," Thomas confirmed. "They bake well with parsnips and lard."

Braddon smiled and held out his hand. "Would you like a tour, Miss Bertha?"

She should wait for Mamma to return, and cast a glance back to the estate.

As if reading her mind, Thomas said, "I'll direct your Ma when she comes back out." Then he set to digging over a nearby garden bed.

Bertha made a calculated confession. "You were winking at me at dinner. A butler should not do that towards a guest who may soon wed his master."

Braddon stumbled. At first his expression indicated he was about to deny it, then his shoulders slumped. "It appears you have uncovered my secret," he said.

Bertha beamed. "That you are so recently appointed? Yes, but you confirmed that yourself." Confidence warmed her. They were making a connection at last.

Braddon looked taken aback. "Ah, yes, obviously."

Bertha stopped walking, "This is no secret at all. All the guests know how hastily arranged this party is, and how recently assembled the staff. We are talking in circles."

Braddon nodded and looked away.

Something odd was happening here. "There is another secret. Is there not?" Bertha asked.

"What? Of course not."

Emboldened, Bertha pushed her luck. "What's wrong with-?"

Braddon said, " -There is nothing wrong with the marquess, I guarantee that."

"What an odd thing to volunteer. How would you know whether this is true or not, being so new to the position that ..." Bertha trailed off. The color drained from her face. She checked her surroundings. They were quite alone.

"Everything is all right," Braddon said suddenly.

"It's you."

"What do you possibly- ?"

" -You're him!"

"Please keep it down."

"You winked at me, deliberately, as if making fun at my expense."

"I should not have, that was indecorous of me. I beg your forgiveness Miss Collingwood."

"Now you're retreating into formality, My Lord?" The pulse rang in Bertha's ears. "You're the marquess, aren't you? Not the crinkled old ... oh my goodness, he's the butler after all. That's why he was counting the silver. That's what a butler does!"

The pieces fell into place, everything suddenly made sense.

"Please do not let on. I beg of you." The Marquess of Hadlow grabbed Bertha by the shoulders. His eyes bored into her soul. Such mesmerizing, beautiful eyes.

Braddon - no - that wasn't his name any more. The marquess said, "I beg of you, keep your discovery to yourself."

"But -" Despite the cool temperature, heat roared through Bertha's system. "I have revealed my plans to you. I told you I wished to get closer to the marquess, little knowing I was speaking directly to him. I am indeed foolish to have spoken so candidly. What a great disaster this is."

"No, Miss Collingwood, it is not a disaster. It is a boon."

"How so?"

"We may talk without suspicion, that is an excellent outcome from this subterfuge. For example, if the mammas in there knew my true identity, I would never get a moment's rest from their scheming."

"That's to your advantage," Bertha said. "Not to *mine*. I told you my mamma has already secured a special license. You must think us fools."

"Would you be heartbroken to learn your mamma is not alone in that endeavor?"

"I...pardon?" Then they were all fools. And they were chasing the wrong man.

"There are at least three young ladies here whose mammas have schemed the same thing. Each thinks they have outfoxed the others."

"You're enjoying yourself." Bertha accused.

"Not in the least. At this very moment I need your discretion and wisdom. There are eyes upon us and if your behavior changes suddenly, it will raise suspicion."

Pulse pounding in her ears, Bertha turned her head to the closest garden bed and pointed at it. "Cabbages."

"Is that what ladies are saying these days for -"

"Growing here. They're cabbages. And next to them are celery, and I believe the flowers planted in between them are marigolds."

Their backs were turned to the estate windows now, so if anyone was looking, they would not see how red of face Bertha appeared now. Her heat could power the glasshouse beds at this very moment. "Why have you and the marquess... no... you *are* the marquess. Why did you change places with the butler?"

Keeping his voice low, Braddon said, "Here comes Thomas."

Bertha too kept her volume in check. "He is not aware of your deception?"

"None of the staff are, except Braddon my faithful retainer. I find I am now in your mercy for your continued discretion."

Bertha inwardly beamed. "Then you must stop winking at me, for that is what alerted me to your lack of suitability as a butler in the first place."

"I must apologize for my lapse. Sometimes the candlelight is too bright and I am not ... it does not matter. We are not at liberty to speak." Then he walked away from Bertha towards the groundskeeper and raised his voice. "Sterling work here with the cabbages and marigolds. The marquess is delighted with the productivity." The men wandered off towards another garden building, Bertha no longer able to discern their conversation.

Mamma appeared, wearing a warmer coat. "Did you learn anything about the marquess from the butler, my dear?"

"A little," Bertha said.

"Pray tell me all, once we are safely back inside. I feel the cold so terribly these days."

Confusion swirled. How did she explain these goings on, when she could barely make sense of it herself? The marquess had asked for her discretion. She would give him the benefit of that, at least.

But for how long?

After a couple of false starts, in which her Mamma blew out her breath even louder to emphasize her impatience, Bertha settled on: "There isn't much to tell, only that the butler and the marquess are both so new to their roles, they have little idea of what to do."

"That's excellent, because the two of you can learn together."

Bertha had to stay out in the cool wind until she regained her equilibrium. "Mamma, I find myself curiously enchanted by these gardens. I shall remain and become familiar with the estate. You take yourself inside now and keep warm."

Her Mamma made a little moue with her mouth in response. Then tisked audibly. "Young people today, they want to do everything differently. I don't know what the world is coming to."

"There you go, exaggerating again," Bertha playfully tapped Mamma's elbow. "I did not mean you should depart so suddenly, we should take a turn in the gardens while the weather remains fair. Who would believe the beds could be so productive at this cold time of year?"

Many of the beds had cloches to keep the heat in, and another garden bed appeared to have sand instead of soil. "Whoever looks after this is talented indeed. I do believe these are- "

Mamma yawned noisily, "My dear, you are trying too hard to impress the wrong person. Come inside into the warm where the ladies are encouraging the marquess to join them for tea."

Excellent, that meant the doddery butler would be somewhere inside the estate, and the real marquess was out here in the gardens. "I'd best tell the butler to attend his master then," Bertha said by way of farewell.

He mother tisked again and strode back towards Hadlow Hall, Bertha took off in the other direction. As she did so, she passed another small building with steamed windows. She was fairly sure it was known as a hotbed. What could they be growing in there? As she reached the door, she heard a sharp cry and a gasp. Then a shuddering sob. Utterly bizarre. Was someone in pain? She reached for the door and saw the shape of two people. It was hard to make out their faces, but it was definitely two people, one a woman with her skirts up around her stomach, and the other was ...oh goodness, it was another woman, kneeling before her!

Bertha froze in shock and wonder, pulled her hand back

from the door handle and hoped to blazes the fog on the glass was thick enough to disguise her own identity.

Goodness, she wasn't the only one here with secrets.

Her shock soon turned to calculated relief. Being utterly mercenary about the situation, this discovery meant two less hearts competing for the marquess's.

She walked briskly in another direction, until somebody called her name. A male voice. "Has something frightened you?"

It was the butler. No, not the butler, the marquess *pretending* to be the butler. This was getting ridiculously confusing.

"I shall still call you Braddon, although it is not your name. The real butler pretending to be you is about to be descended upon and implored to take tea with the rest of the ladies." Then she recalled what she had only recently witnessed and corrected herself, "Most of the ladies."

"You will not be there?" He asked

"Stop," she shook her head. "What I mean is, *you* need to be in there."

He made no move to rescue his elderly retainer. "No I don't, that's exactly why we swapped roles. So those ladies in their frills and layers of lace would not set upon me."

"If you didn't want to be around the guests, you should have swapped roles with your outdoor staff. Or at the very least an equerry. A butler's absence from the party will be noted, and commented upon."

"I doubt it. I don't exist to them."

"On the contrary. The absence of key staff and lack of attention to detail will be noted. It's a sign of a poorly-run estate. After all, if I noticed, they will notice, and then your whimsical game shall come undone."

He shook his head as if to continue arguing with her. Then he stopped. "I'm a marquess you know, I can do what I damn well please."

"Indeed."

He grinned at her, making something flurry in her chest.

He continued, "You shall treat me with the respect I am due."

Bertha grinned in conspiracy. "A marquess pretending to be a butler, who doesn't want anyone to know he's a marquess … will receive the respect he *truly* is due."

He leaned back and laughed to the sky. As he turned and looked at Bertha again, something behind her caught his eye.

Bertha spun around to see what he was looking at. There were two ladies exiting the hot-beds.

The marquess said, "I wonder what they were looking for in there?"

"Don't let them see us," Bertha grabbed his hand and pulled him towards a potting shed. "I mean, you." She swiftly corrected. Immediately she dropped his hand. What was wrong with her, placing her hands on his person like that? "I do apologize."

"Miss Collingwood, no apology necessary." He reached for her hand and held it in his. His knuckles showed old scars.

"How did you get those?" She traced the lines with her thumb. "And why in heaven's name are you no longer wearing gloves? You had them on a moment ago?"

He made a deep sigh. "The French campaign. Always better to ride without gloves, gives you better control of the reigns and the horse holding my fate. I got used to not wearing them."

"You were at Waterloo?"

He nodded, but said nothing more.

"You're right about one thing," Bertha acquiesced, "Pretending to be the butler will keep you safe for longer. If the ladies inside knew you were the real marquess, and a war hero at that, they would eat you alive. You'd be wishing yourself back on the battlefields."

"Clearly, you can see my predicament?"

"Alas, yes. But can you also see mine? My exclamation last evening at dinner has rather shown my hand."

"Shown your honesty, you mean. The other young ladies were looking at my retainer like a prize specimen. The man could barely feed himself, such were his shakes, and yet they completely overlooked that because they thought he was the marquess."

Bertha giggled, "I can imagine being sized-up by a room full of eligible debutantes and their scheming mammas would make any man tremble. But it is an unfair game you play, at the ladies' expense."

With the coast clear, they continued to walk through the garden beds, stopping to enjoy the aromas of herbs she crushed between her fingers. The mint was running wild, no need to conserve that, but there was also a good deal of tarragon. She caressed the leaves, releasing the fragrance.

"I lied before, I did wink." he confessed.

"I knew it! Why did you flirt so outrageously with me?"

"Because you'd sized up the old man and I wanted to know if you could be misdirected."

Bertha dropped the tarragon. "In what way?" The conversation was about to take a turn for the worse, she could feel it.

"I needed to ascertain whether you would marry the marquess just for the title, and then, once he died, find your own ... ah ... entertainments."

How dare he insult her like that? "I ... excuse me ... you do not speak to ladies like that my lord, it is most unbecoming. You insult every lady under your roof with such an accusation."

At which point, Mamma came around the corner and gasped. "Oh my heavens! Bertha, get away from the butler right this minute. You didn't come here to have an affair with the help!"

CHAPTER 4

The sun shone weakly through the window as the maids opened the drapes the next morning. Light snow had fallen across the gardens, but the heavy clouds had long gone, leaving everything dusted in a layer of magic. The sunlight, low in the sky, bounced off the untouched white ground. It was so bright Bertha had to shield her eyes, although there was no heat in it.

It was time to make an appearance at breakfast and rejoin the house party.

In the breakfast room, they found several gentlemen and the butler-in-marquess's-clothing chatting amiably about potential activities. Bertha loved the far-more relaxed customs of breakfast. Assemble what you like from the servers, no rules about where one may sit, or with whom to talk. She and Mamma sat and ate, while the gentlemen chatted amongst themselves.

It was so odd that the dinners were such formal occasions, and yet the breakfasts were something of a free-for all.

Perhaps because most of the ladies were engaged in their regular correspondences and had not yet come down?

Had she made another misstep again? Nobody was gasping or rushing her from the room, so Bertha guessed no. It did seem odd that if their aim of being at the house party was to secure a husband, or make connections, as her family fervently hoped she did, why were the rest of the ladies not down here at breakfast, securing husbands and making connections?

A maid entered the room, piled some toast and preserves onto a plate, then placed the plate on a tray. Then they added a pot of tea and cup and saucer to the tray, then sat a cloche over it and walked out.

Taking it to their mistress, no doubt.

Possibly what Mary and Mamma should have done. The gentlemen were still talking, but their voices were exceptionally muted and intended not to be overheard.

It was one thing to study the rules, as they were set down. Bertha wasn't bragging when she acknowledged what a good study she made. She had learned the rules and applied them.

But how did one learn the *unwritten* rules of society?

Not even the Wollstonecraft book she adored had an answer for that.

She tucked into her egg and sipped her chocolate, ruminating on the unfair nature of it all, when the most wonderful thing happened. The butler-marquess sat down with a plate of food, not two seats away! Definitely within talking distance, although there was a vacant chair between them. She wasn't making a play for him, even if he had been the real thing. She merely wished to convey that she was in no way attempting to compromise him.

And then Mamma, pretending to get herself another coffee, physically stood up and removed the chair between her and the Butler-marquess. She placed the seat by the fire and called another of the gentlemen over to not only get her a coffee, but to come and sit by the fire and keep her company for a moment!

Too polite to refuse, the man known as George Wellingbourne brought the coffee pot over and refilled Mamma's cup. Then he pulled up a chair and sat!

Mamma smiled deeply at him and blinked several times.

Was she ... flirting with him! Honestly, Mamma!

The butler turned to Bertha and asked, "How are you enjoying Surrey, Miss Collingwood?"

"It is truly lovely," she said, then suddenly remembered to add, "My lord," to keep up the pretense that he was in fact the marquess.

He'd noticed. The expression of shock that rippled over his face. One had to concentrate to see it, and Bertha was sure it was only she who had seen it, but seen it she had.

Keeping her voice low, she leaned closer to him and said, "My lord, your secret is safe with me."

Alas, the leaning in was too close. Their chairs, such a distance apart, were more than was usual around a table. Mamma, who just happened to be walking past, accidentally tipped Bertha's chair just that bit closer.

Bertha lurched forward, unable to stop. She flung her arms out to break her fall. Gravity pulled her closer to the mock marquess.

Somehow, through absolutely no fault of her own, her body crashed into his, and his face met hers.

Everybody in the room gasped at the sight of Miss Collingwood and Lord Hadlow in a sudden embrace.

"Oh my stars!" Mamma proclaimed, I had no idea the marquess had developed such a tendre for my darling Bertha that he would cast all propriety aside in such a fashion!"

Bertha extricated herself from the poor retainer, who looked just as flummoxed and embarrassed as she. "Mamma, please, that's not what happened. I merely lost my balance."

"But my darling, there are so many witnesses! There is only one way this can end now, obviously. It's just as well I secured the special license!"

At which point the man dressed as the butler, but who was truly the real marquess, entered the breakfast room. "What's all this?"

Bertha pleaded with the Lord above to make this horrible scene disappear. But there would be no such good fortune. "It's all a misunderstanding, no harm done." She tried again. "Perhaps you might help the marquess recover his dignity, and fetch him a clean set of clothes, as his current lot appear to be covered in hot chocolate."

Mamma was having none of it, "Bertha dear, you've been slighted, I'll not have it, not with so many witnesses. We all saw what we saw."

It was time for Bertha to leave her breakfast, even though she'd much rather eat another egg, as they were done to perfection. She stood up and said to the room, "My lords, good sirs, I apologize for the disruption. Please don't let what happened here color your opinion of my dear Mamma or of myself. I ... I feel a headache coming on, and I must retire. Good morning to you all."

Walking out of the room, she passed the "butler" and gave him a look that she hoped he would read as, "Your secret is safe with me, but your real butler might not be safe from Mamma."

CHAPTER 5

The sun, although weak, shone brightly the next day. The perfect opportunity to engage in a picnic. Provided the rugs were thick enough and they dressed warmly.

Bertha wore her warmest everything to join in the "pleasantries" outside. It felt incredibly silly to be venturing out of doors at this time of year, but the marquess deemed they should engage in a "Hunt for Treasures."

The men and women were divided into four groups, two groups of men, two of women. Bertha's competitive spirit kicked in as she read the list of "treasures" to be found.

It began in the pinery, which delighted all gathered. What a marvelous way to enjoy the outdoors, even though they were walled in and the roof was domed with glass. So lovely and warm. And light.

Here, raised beds of fruits grew, even in winter. There were orange trees, with large green fruit that were nowhere near ready for picking. But that didn't matter, as she'd spotted a lime as well – although come to think of it, how did the limes look any different to the oranges at this time of year?

And then she saw it, the first clue on a list of treasured items.

Something to pine for.

This is where the pinery received its name. The marquess was growing actual pineapples. Produce from the tropics, growing here in southern England! Bertha had heard about similar exploits produced by a Duke in Scotland, but she'd never seen it for herself.

The ladies in Bertha's group gasped at the sight of the tall, spiked grasses sitting in their pots, buried deep in chunks of bark. There, in the middle of each grass nest, grew the smallest, most adorable pineapples. Utterly green and not ready for picking at all, how were they to take the item to the marquess without destroying it?

Katherine asked, "Should we lift it out, including the pot?"

Mary said, "Would that harm the roots, perhaps? I wouldn't want to disturb them."

Katherine considered this. "We'd get our clothes dirty."

Bertha suggested, "I'm more concerned about gashing my face against those spiked leaves."

Mary said, "We could gather a pine cone instead?"

Ah yes, but that meant braving the true outdoor weather, instead of this protected space. Could there be another way?

The pineapple bush was so spiky, defending its precious baby in the center, they didn't dare approach it lest they cut themselves or their clothing.

"I have it," Katherine said. "The one we pine for is the marquess, so let's grab him!"

The rest of the ladies readily agreed and darted off to the center of the picnic area, giggling at their target.

They grabbed the elderly gentleman standing beside the true marquess, and declared themselves the champions of finding the first clue.

"We declare that we pine for you, My Lord!" Katherine said.

Bertha cast a shy look towards the marquess-in-butler's-clothing and caught a wink in return. She blushed.

The other teams had darted outside and gathered a sprig of pine needles, and the men had outdone themselves and pulled out an entire pine sapling, roots and all. They cheered themselves on as if they'd slain a mammoth from ancient times.

Next challenge required they find "Something to cheer for."

This was more puzzling. What brought good cheer? The ladies puzzled over this for a little longer.

Boyed by their success with the "pining", Katherine suggested they grab the marquess again. But then the marquess – or at least his butler – declared it had to be something different each time.

They spent so long debating what they could find to cheer for that the gentlemen of the party completely beat them to it. They found beer brewing in vats and poured themselves a couple of tankards. When they returned, they charged those tankards and cheered their good fortune.

"Oh bother," Bertha said, disliking this strange, new anger coursing through her. Who knew she was so competitive after all?

They had to win the next challenge. Even though there was no prize. Ah, but then she realized there was a prize – it had to be to show the marquess, the real one, how clever she was. He didn't want a simpering wife who would agree to anything he said. He wanted someone who might challenge him from time to time. Someone who could think for herself.

Or at least, she hoped as much. Otherwise this entire entreaty would come to naught.

Their third clue: Something modest.

Oh, such sneaky clue. How could one be modest if one also wanted to win this competition? If a person was to declare themselves modest, would that not also be a brag of sorts, and therefore render the modesty null and void?

"Ladies, what should we do?" Katherine said.

"Something modest," Elizabeth ruminated.

"It's a trick," Bertha said. "Let's think of something clever. He wants to confuse us. But we shall prevail."

"What about soil?" Katherine said.

By Jove, she was right! "That's brilliant, Katherine! Soil is the best idea. And we are surrounded by it. Excellent thinking. Now, how shall we present it?"

They could not insert their hands into the soil without getting exceedingly dirty. And yet, soil had to be the right answer.

The gentlemen were cheering at something they'd found outside. Oh dear, the ladies were running out of time.

"Katherine, hold your hands together like this," Bertha made a cupping motion. She saw a small trowel and used it to dig a little soil from the garden bed and tip it into Katherine's hand.

"Oh no, I can't!" Katherine said. "Just keep it on the trowel. We shall all become frightfully dirty."

"But the trowel is far too decorative. It needs to be in our hands for modesty," Bertha said. She took her gloves off and directed Elizabeth to pour the soil into her cupped palm. A worm wriggled in the soil in Bertha's palm.

"Oh!" Katherine yelped. "I may faint."

"No, don't you see?" Bertha beamed. "This is perfect! A modest worm. It's the hardest working creature of all. Good gardens need worms to grow. I read that in father's news sheet."

"Your father is in trade?" Katherine asked.

"Indeed he is. And dare I say, he's made a "modest fortune" in the news sheet trade."

Walking carefully so as not to disturb the soil and the worm, they walked towards the marquess and his butler. The gentlemen came barreling in and ran past them, with their modest discovery and beat them to the finish line.

Drat!

They'd lost after all.

But ho, the marquess declared charging ahead and beaming with pride were not at all modest, and gave the gentlemen a penalty. It did seem as if he were making up the rules as he went along. Oh well, his house party, his rules.

Bertha stepped forward. "If it pleases, my lord, may I present a modest sod of earth."

"That is indeed modest," the faux marquess said. He held out a plate and Bertha deposited the soil on it. At which point, it exposed the worm, wriggling and flicking in the exposed air. "And even more modest than soil, is the creation that lives within it, working ceaselessly for no reward. The most modest of all God's creations, the worm."

"Well played, Ladies, well played indeed." The fake marquess said. "I declare the ladies have won."

The gentlemen took the defeat in good grace, applauding their ingenuity and congratulating them.

Once indoors again, the ladies retired to their rooms and the gentlemen did whatever gentlemen did at a house party when they were at liberty to do whatever they desired.

With all the exertion, Mamma directed Bertha to take a bath. She set the maids to hauling buckets of hot water into the tub.

Mamma put scented oils in the water, and it truly smelled divine.

"You did beautifully today. I was entirely vexed with you after breakfast, when you contradicted my claims. But I see now you have a better plan to win the marquess. I only wish you would hurry up and secure his hand."

The warm, scented water provided solace for Bertha. Her mother tested her nerves at times. "Mamma, what else do we do at house parties, aside from eat and play games?"

"Playing games is the entire point. Today the Marques was testing your resolve, your ingenuity, your very essence. I truly did enjoy watching you working out the puzzles. You shone, my dear. Even in the modesty stakes. I am, dare I say it, hopeful you truly have earned your coronet."

Yes, the coronet. That was the entire point of being here. Well, she had done that, but of course, her Mamma had no idea what was really going on. For a moment of madness, Bertha thought about telling her Mamma who the real marquess was. But then she thought better of it. Why ruin the fun? She knew who the real marquess was, and that was all that mattered. And if she told her Mamma, her Mamma would no doubt expose the fake marquess and demand the real one reveal himself.

Bertha's was the true path. It provided opportunity for her and the real marquess to understand each other a little more, instead of being rushed into Parson's Noose.

And the other ladies and their Mammas could make as many doe-eyes as they liked at the doddery old butler.

She still didn't think it was fair on the rest of the ladies though. They were setting their eyes on the wrong prize.

Should she tell them?

Would they hate her or thank her for the information?

The longer the charade lasted, the harder it would be to reveal the real marquess. She shouldn't string the rest of the ladies along like this. They deserved to know too, did they not? Then they too could get to know him properly, and be able to make their own decision about whether they'd be a good match.

The hot water soaked her muscles and she found herself relaxing. She really should reveal the marquess's secret. And yet ...somehow she couldn't bring herself to do it.

Something else gnawed at her conscience ... the truth of the situation was, she didn't actually want to.

Oh dear. Reality kicked the truth at her. She wanted the real marquess to herself!

CHAPTER 6

The gentlemen were out hunting or ... doing whatever gentlemen did at a house party in winter. Bertha sat in the library late one afternoon, sitting near the fire for its warmth and glowing light, so she may read one of the books from her room.

It was rather lovely to have staff bring in tea when she rang, but for the rest of the time she was quite alone and able to enjoy the momentary serenity.

After all, these might be the last few moments of peace and quiet before her life moved from the world of her parents to the world of her new husband. The other ladies and their Mammas and chaperones were elsewhere, possibly in their rooms, planning what to wear for dinner.

From a side door, she heard the sound of footsteps.

"That's fine, I don't need -" she began to say, and then stopped. It wasn't a maid with another pot of tea. It was the marquess, dressed once more as the butler.

"Thought I'd find you here," he said, a cheeky grin on his

face. "Some of the other ladies are taking afternoon tea. But you are not."

"I am engaging in that most disagreeable habit of modern women; reading."

"However will society cope if women keep educating themselves this way?"

Despite the interruption, a smile crept over her face. "I do so love to read." Would he take the hint and leave her to her reading?

"As do I," he said, taking a seat nearby and clearly answering her unasked question in the negative. He would not be leaving her alone.

He unfolded a news sheet and Bertha recognized it as her father's publication.

"Let's see what scandals are unfolding in the courts, shall we?" He said.

"Oh yes, let's," Bertha readily agreed. She placed a slip of paper in the page she was up to and closed her book, then gave her full attention to the marquess. "What is the latest on our King and need to be rid of our Queen Caroline?"

"You possibly know more than I, being privy to the details."

"I assure you, I am not. I only know what is printed, not what cannot be. And in any case, surely the King should not be pursuing divorce during this most holy time of year?"

"Whose side are you on then, my dear, The King's or The Queen's?"

"Naturally, I am taking Queen Caroline's side. Although I do not for one moment condone her behavior."

"You would seek to champion a foreigner over our natural-born King?"

Bertha smiled at the challenge in his question. "It is a lively debate, and the future of the country is at stake. And yes, the very issue is proving a boon for my family's business. The Caller is our family newssheet and is highly sought in the coffee houses all through London. And you yourself have a copy. For me, the central issue is that the King, whoever he should be, should not throw his wife aside as a matter of convenience. It would set a terrible precedent."

Then she remembered her history lessons.

"Well, what I mean is, it would set another terrible precedent. We all know what happened the last time the Monarch sought a divorce."

"True, true," The marquess smiled, enjoying their private conversation. "But even your father's news sheet explains that the scandalous behavior in which she has engaged cannot be borne, especially by a King?"

Bertha shot back, "His behavior is no better."

The marquess shrugged, "He is the King, he can do as he likes."

Bertha wasn't having that. "Would you behave in such a way?"

"I am not the king."

"But now that everybody knows how poorly the King has treated his Queen, what kind of example does he set? It is true you are not the king." She dropped her voice low, just in case anyone should walk in, "But you are a marquess. Would you do the same to your future wife, with the excuse that if It's good enough for the King, It's good enough for you?"

He gave it some thought and stared into the fire for a time. "Perhaps, if your father's newssheet had not made such a public debacle of the entire affair, nobody outside court circles would know."

Bertha had heard this accusation before, in various discussions in the coffee houses. The King's scandal was proving an excellent business opportunity. Readers and listeners could not get enough of the details pertaining to the King and Queen, and their admissions in public of how they had conducted their affairs during the regency. The Queen had spent much of her marriage on the continent, and had barely been in the public consciousness. Indeed, it had been the newssheets, like The Caller and others, who had let the public know their queen was even back in the country at all.

Without newssheets disseminating information, it was unlikely that anybody would even realize their King was trying to divorce. The last time a king had divorced, the country was torn asunder. Perhaps that's why so many had taken Caroline's side? She was hardly a sympathetic figure. Reading about her behavior always reddened Bertha's cheeks. She'd read sections out aloud in the coffee houses, and felt her face burn at the contents.

And that was the material they could print!

She squirmed to think what else had been going on.

"It's true, reports of royal events is where my fortune is secured. People cannot get enough of the scandal. At present we are at a lull in proceedings, but I have every confidence they will pick up again in the new year, and the public will want to know what their King is attempting. Thus, my family's fortune will grow. And, if I may be so bold, that is the entire reason I'm here. I'm worth, conservatively, more than the rest of the eligible ladies here combined."

"That sounds remarkably cold-blooded and businesslike," he said, examining something on his fingernail.

"What is, my dear marquess? The discussion of money or the subject of marriage and divorce?"

He looked up at her, but remained silent.

She filled the gap. "It amuses me so. I have sought the best advice on how to behave at a house party, as my decorum is under scrutiny at all times. However, the very reason I am here, or that any of us are here at all, for that matter, is something we are not supposed to mention at all. Which to me seems counter-productive."

"In what way?"

If we cannot talk about the subject of marriage, let alone divorce. And if we are hardly ever mixing company and making connections to find out if we would ever be agreeable with each other, how are we ever able to actually brooch the topic at all, and make any such successful arrangements? Obviously there are many eligible ladies here who are keen to secure a husband. And the gentlemen here ... I am not sure what to think – are they seeking wives or are they here simply to help you?"

"I did not want to interrupt your flow, but Miss Collingwood, we are indeed talking and mixing company right now. I find you, if not yet agreeable, at least diverting. Perhaps even challenging."

"Well, yes, but we are only in company because you are incognito."

He bristled. "If I had not been, we would never have had the opportunity to gain an understanding of each other. And so, it rather seems that this is more for *your* benefit."

"Truly?" She didn't believe him.

"Indeed. None of the other ladies have paid me the slightest attention."

"How long will you subject your poor, sweet butler to their whims? The man deserves a medal of valor for enduring this party."

"Yes. I should rescue him. The poor man has probably had so much tea his back teeth are floating."

Bertha laughed so heartily she dropped her book.

CHAPTER 7

Leopold - he'd have to get used to using his whole name again instead of Leo, as he'd used in the regiment - wouldn't exactly call Miss Collingwood's laugh gracious. Or musical. It had the volume and caliber of nearby gunfire, and for the briefest moment, he felt himself back in the campaign.

Except he was not fighting Napoleon's troops in a muddy field. He was in a comfortable room with a warm fire; a welcome change indeed. To add to the warmth and comfort, he had a beautiful young woman with whom to converse.

A beautiful woman who had kept his secret.

A not unwelcome development, to be certain. For the little time he'd known her, he'd found Miss Collingwood to at least be trustworthy. Along with her other assets; her pleasing countenance, and, he had to admit, the blunt.

A terrible thing, the marriage campaign. The poor waifs thrown in his butler's direction were little more than cannon fodder.

He chose not to interrupt Miss Collingwood's perfor-mance, rather enjoying her opinions.

"... and so we are all pretending that we are attending a party with no ulterior motive other than to partake in enjoying past times, and yet you desperately need a well-heeled wife otherwise the estate and everyone in it will starve."

He realize she'd stopped, so he supposed he should say something. Just as he was about to suggest something, she continued, which was convenient.

"You do need to marry, and as I have the greatest assets, it appears I'm your best opportunity. What a shame we are never allowed to discuss such things."

He really should rescue Braddon. Heaven knows what sort of trouble the young ladies had him in. But he found himself unable to leave. "There are a great many things we are not supposed to talk about, Miss Collingwood, and I would hazard a guess money is at the very top of that list."

"Indeed," she said, "And yet money is the most important thing, is it not, in your selection criteria for a wife and future Marchioness? You have Hadlow Hall to maintain, after all."

"That does appear to be the case. However, money can't be everything, can it?" Oh dear, now his mouth was running away with him. "It would be convenient if there was some attraction bundled into the package."

"Attraction?"

"Yes. A spark, so to speak." He reached for her hand. There was nobody else here to stop them, because nobody else had a clue who he was. So convenient. He really shouldn't be so brazen, but it had been so very long since he'd had anything more than a conversation with a charming young lady. "An ability to speak, rather than simper, is vitally important. And if the future Marchioness were somewhat attractive, that would make the begetting of heirs a great deal more advantageous."

She did not remove her hand from his, and he found himself caressing her palm with his thumb.

She pinked, but kept up her end of the conversation. "That topic is something else we're not supposed to talk about, and yet it is also a vitally important thing. You need heirs, otherwise there will be yet another long search for an heir."

He raised her hand towards his face. Any moment now she would withdraw it, but he could not let her go. "If you were at liberty to speak about it, if you hadn't studied so many manners, what would your opinion be on the, ah, begetting of heirs?" He'd surely crossed the line now.

"Well," Bertha swallowed.

There was nobody else in the library. Nobody was listening in. Nobody else knew about their conversations - either here or in the gardens. She was intoxicating and quite beguiling.

She gifted him a smile. "If I were at liberty to speak of begetting heirs, I would also be inclined towards a husband who was also somewhat attractive. That would make the task more ... bearable."

"Bearable?" He kissed her lace-gloved palm. Why did women wear gloves so often? The dratted things made movement so awkward.

She blinked at the onslaught, but made no more to get closer or withdraw. "I must confess, I do not fully understand the machinations but I'm led to believe there is a need for a great deal of kissing."

He nearly choked.

"Is there not? I was rather looking forward to that part of the marriage bargain."

"There is indeed a great deal of kissing required," he confirmed. He kissed her palm again, and then again as he moved to the end of her lace glove. Then he pushed the cuff of that annoying fabric away with his finger and kissed the pulse at her wrist.

The made the slowest blink he thought he imagined it. Then another of her beatific smiles.

"I do thank you for your candor. You see, although I am under instructions ..." She started counting on the fingers of her free hand "...to only discuss the weather, needlework, cooking and the latest mode of fashion, these are things that can only occupy me for at most ten minutes. There is so much more that I want to discuss, and now that I have spoken of my desires, I believe that is something else I should like to have in a husband. The ability to speak freely of the things of which I'm most ...curious."

A bullet could not have stopped his heart faster. He kissed her wrist again, his blood pooling away from his head towards something else. "Curiosity is a maligned quality in a human," Leo said. "However, I esteem it most highly. I must confess, if more of the guests this week had displayed a stronger vein of curiosity, they may have discovered my ruse, just as you have."

She smiled and gently withdrew her hand from his and folded her arms together in her lap. "Are you of a mind to disabuse the ladies before this party is over?"

Honesty blurted forth. "Oh, goodness me no. Why would I spoil the fun and do that?"

Bertha shrugged as she retrieved her book and stood up. He stood as well. "Honesty is a very attractive feature in any person. I do not believe I could make a happy marriage with anybody of the dishonest persuasion."

He reached for her arm but she avoided him. "Are you going to reveal my deception?"

He earned a shake of her head. "I would not, it is not my role to unburden you of the guilt you must be positively drowning in by now."

With that she departed, leaving Leopold alone with his conscience.

CHAPTER 8

The next afternoon, the ladies were making the sweetest fuss over the old butler.

Mamma kicked Bertha's heels as if to say, "Get over there and make him fall in love with you."

Bertha no longer felt the need to participate in the grand deception. "I may have a headache coming on, Mamma."

"You can't, you're not due for another five days."

Not that sort of headache," Bertha said. "Consider this a bonus headache that crept up on me. Possibly from each of the ladies here wearing a different scent."

"Have another tea." Mamma advised. "Sweet hot tea is excellent for headaches."

"I shall retire to our rooms. I'm sure my headache will be gone in time for dinner."

Mamma stood up to accompany her.

"You don't have to come. I shall be fine after a short lie down, that is all."

"Nonsense darling, I feel something of a headache coming on myself."

Oh dear, she didn't want the company. But if she argued, everyone would want to know what was going on. So Mamma followed.

As they reached the stairs, Bertha asked her mother again if she would rather return to the drawing room with the marquess.

"I am your chaperone, and I must make sure to deliver you to your room."

"Why would I require that?" There was nobody else around. Nobody to overhear them.

Mamma hastened them to their room, dismissed their maids and closed the door. "I know you feel some attraction with the butler, but my darling, I'm here to assure you nothing can come from such an alliance. At least, not until after you are safely wed to the marquess and produce an heir. What you do after that is of no concern."

The memory of the marquess's kisses branded her wrist and heat spread over her face. "It's not what you think, Mamma." Was all she felt at liberty to say.

What a mess. Mamma hadn't noticed the butler wasn't really a butler at all. Yet she'd more or less promised the marquess not to reveal his secret.

Mamma put her hands on her hips, elbows akimbo. "It is exactly what I think. You cannot be seen with the staff. It's one thing to be thankful for having good help, It's another entirely to cause the absolutely wrong kind of scandal with them. You're here to get the marquess of Hadlow to compromise you, not compromise yourself with a workman with absolutely no future."

"I truly do have a headache," Bertha said, telling the truth.

At dinner, Bertha found herself sitting further away from

the man-who-pretended to be the marquess. And yet, to her inner delight, she was seated much closer to where the butler stood, as he guided the footmen in and out with trays of food. Mamma sat a few seats away, closer to the make-do-marquess. The real marquess must have had something to do with the seating arrangements, to mix things around like this.

It truly wasn't the done thing, to rearrange the seating arrangements in such a way. Even Bertha knew this was incorrect and a terrible breach of protocol. Yet she couldn't help feeling delighted. No doubt people would complain, but not within earshot of the man they thought was the marquess.

The ladies, if they noticed, said nothing about their changed arrangements. Instead, they praised the meal, the cooking and the service. The doddery old man sitting in the marquess's chair at the head of the table raised his glass each time somebody made a compliment.

Later, as the maids helped them out of their evening gowns, Mamma said, "I told you to remain at afternoon tea. Now you have completely fallen out of favor with the marquess. You must work even harder to get on his sweet side. Put on your night gown, I have a plan."

"Mamma, dinner was lovely. And anyway, there's nothing wrong with wanting to move the seating around. That way we all get to sit with different guests and have different conversations."

"That's as may be. But he could not have seated you so far from him. You must have displeased him in some way. We shall go to him at once. Fetch the good brandy."

"What are we doing?"

"We are going to him. We shall say he looked pale at dinner and have brought him some medicinal brandy. He will accept it, then you shall allow your night gown to slip past your shoulder. I shall catch him in the act and demand he marry you."

"Mamma, don't you think that is a little extreme?"

"I do not. We depart in three days and we must do something before that coronet slips through our hands."

"Our hands?"

"Your hands. Come along."

Barely a minute later, Bertha stood outside the marquess's door. Mamma stood beside her, holding a silver tray with a decanter of brandy and some glass tumblers. Exactly how Mamma knew it was the marquess's door puzzled Bertha.

Mamma tilted her head at the door and hissed, "Stop wasting time!"

Bertha knocked at the door and the old retainer opened it. He too was wearing a long night shirt under a loosely slung flannel gown. Bertha couldn't help thinking if he were a real marquess, he'd have a silk one instead.

Mamma did all the talking.

"We were concerned you may not be feeling quite well, My Lord, so have come to offer you a post-prandial digestive."

"Oh! That's ... most kind. Ah, let me ..."

"Don't mind us," Mamma said, letting herself into his rooms. She set the tray down on an ottoman near the fire and poured him a glass. "Come and sit by the fire, My Lord." Then instead of handing him the glass, she called Bertha over. "Dearest, give the marquess his drink."

Bertha had given up trying to deduce her Mamma's reason for such double handling, and reached for the glass. She turned and gave it to the marquess, who had taken his seat. As he took the glass from her hands, Mamma pushed her in the back, sending her sprawling into the old man's lap.

Mamma shrieked. "Heavens above! Calamity!"

"No, wait, Mamma," Bertha tried to detangle herself, but she had no balance and her feet were in the air. The old retainer spluttered and coughed at the assault and tried to help Bertha to her feet, spilling the brandy in the process.

Arms and legs akimbo, Bertha pushed herself out of the chair and fell at his feet. Her actions had the unfortunate effect of grabbing the old man's collar and pulling it wide open, as if the man was exposing his chest to her.

For her pains, Bertha's dressing gown flapped open and exposed her milky shoulder.

"I've never been so shocked!" Mamma cried out.

At which point, the real marquess, still pretending to be the butler, entered the room. "Is everything in order, only, I heard shouting."

Mamma spoke loudly enough to bring all the guests running to the marquess's door. "Everything is not in order. The marquess has compromised my daughter."

"Mamma, please."

"He has no option, they must wed, otherwise there will be no escaping the scandal."

Bertha wordlessly pleaded with Braddon to set things to rights and explain this disastrous mess.

Braddon, the rotter, merely smiled. "Miss Bertha does appear to be in a fair state of dishabille, and the old man reeks of alcohol. Best move far from the fire, otherwise you'll go up in flames."

"I have the marriage license. the marquess can make all this right the morning after next." Mamma said.

Braddon could have cleared up the confusion. Did he? Most certainly not. He smiled at the scene playing out before him. Mamma's eyes gleamed with victory. Bertha wanted to cry.

"We shall invite all our houseguests to the wedding," Braddon added.

"A marvelous suggestion. Get the house ready for the wedding breakfast!" Mamma said.

Bertha had visions of throwing the lot of them into the fire.

CHAPTER 9

Bertha did not sleep. She lay abed long enough for the entire house to turn quiet. The gentle snuffle coming from Mamma's room told her at least one of them was down for the count.

Slipping on a gown, then slipping out the door, Bertha made her way back to the marquess's rooms. It was one thing to trade professions, but another entirely to trade actual rooms. Her quarry had to be here – otherwise he really had taking this role reversal too far.

Should she knock? That would risk waking others. Who knew how many were asleep in this wing? She turned the handle and her breath hitching as she creaked it open.

Inside the fire still crackled on the hearth, but had reduced in the past hour or so to embers. The marquess, the real one, sat in his real robe and his butler-world's greatest performer stood there in a flannel arrangement, holding a silver tray.

"Ah, Miss Collingwood, I'm grateful you could join us." The real marquess said. "Braddon, please stay, you're in this too."

Bertha wanted to scream. "My lord, we need to call off this farce. We are all agreed this is a terrible misunderstanding that need not go any further."

"But it must." The marquess said. "It's so perfectly perfect, I cannot have imagined a more perfect result to this charade."

"How so?"

He smiled. "Do sit. Braddon, offer the poor girl a drink, she'll need one to keep up her strength for the wedding."

Bertha sat, feeling more confused than ever. "I do not enjoy being your plaything, sir."

"But you enjoy being your Mamma's?"

Bertha looked into the fire for some hope, or inspiration. "That is unfair, she is doing her best. She only wants what's best for me."

"As do all the mammas here, who have all thrown their daughters into Braddon's path. Some more forcefully than others, I should add."

"I'm glad our discomfort has brought you much amusement, sir."

"Ah, but you see, this will work out for the best. You are the only one who has seen through my disguise. You are the most sensible woman here, with – and I lack the grace to say this any other way – an entirely insensible Mamma. If we do not wed, she will drag you through the season like a prize, ready to trap the next unwary baronet. Who, I am sure, will have even less scruples than I."

"How can one have less scruples than pretending to be somebody they are not?"

"That cuts deeply, my dear. But I will take your wrath, if only to call an end to this blasted house party with all the simpering debutantes and demanding Mammas. Do you not see? Once people realize the marquess of Hadlow is married, the whole beribboned lot of them will move on to the next target, and I shall be free to be left alone here in the country, and get my head around what it truly means to be a marquess."

"Why do you not simply tell them all to leave? that this has all been a terrible mistake. That you've changed your mind and will marry a cousin ... from York or ... or anywhere?"

"Hmmm, yes, the beloved in the north is an oft-used ruse. They would never see through that."

Bertha took a deep breath. It did nothing to calm her. "Do you realize ... if I marry Braddon here, my dowry goes to him. A butler. A very loyal and suffering butler, and after everything you have exposed him to, he quite possibly deserves it? And that means you shall remain an impoverished marquess."

"Nonsense," he came and sat near her. "I am the marquess. Your dowry will come to the estate."

"Why are you making me go through with this? I thought ... well, I guess I was a fool, but I foolishly thought ... we were coming to some kind of understanding."

"You are not foolish at all. I do like you very much," The marquess said. "I do believe we could get along rather well."

"As do I." Bertha was more confused than she had ever been. "Which is why I'm so perplexed. I thought we had formed, if not a firm attachment, at least the beginnings of one."

"Indeed, we have, and I appreciate your emotional confession. That settles it. You may call me Leo."

"Leo" Bertha tried out the sound of it. "Leo, please call the wedding off?"

"Goodness no, my dear Bertha, all of this pretending will go to waste if we don't go through with the wedding!"

Bertha turned to Braddon. "Are you going along with this as well?"

Braddon nodded. "I serve at the pleasure of the marquess."

This could not be happening.

Bertha's parents had spared no expense (or privacy) in hastily coordinating the most humiliatingly public wedding at the local parish church. Her father stood with her, ready to guide her down the aisle.

The entire staff, right down to the scullery maids, were waiting outside the doors, clapping and cheering as the doors opened.

Her father held her arm in a vice-like grip and took to the steps, jolting Bertha in the direction of the altar.

Everybody inside the church stood to attention as they came in. One hundred pairs of eyes turned in her direction. Their body heat, mixed with the holly and pine stung her eyes.

Despite her apparent détente with the marquess the evening before, one thing became hideously clear. She and Leo were not the ones getting married today. Everybody here still believed the old butler really was the marquess, and judging by some of the expressions from the ladies in the pews, some of them looked relieved that they were not the bride after all.

There, standing in the groom's position was the marquess's doddery retainer. Standing beside him was Leo the real marquess, still pretending to be the valet. He was going to make her go through with this ridiculous charade? Surely, he'd do something in a moment – swap places and announce to all his real identity?

Come on darling, don't make this last any longer than it has to.

The Vicar stood ready to perform the service. Flies buzzed

in Bertha's ears, which seemed odd for this very cold time of year. Then she realized it was only her pulse hammering away. It blocked out much of what the Vicar said as he welcomed everyone to bear witness to the proceedings.

This can't be happening. It's not happening.

Yet it was.

Her mother, sitting in the front pew, fair beamed at the incredible match she'd orchestrated. If only she knew what a true mess she'd made of things!

The Vicar mentioned Bertha's name and she suddenly paid attention. He spoke her full name, and asked if she was willing to take Leopold John Thaxton Grove, the fourth marquess of Hadlow – he got the full name treatment as well, which took a little longer – as her wedded husband?

Hang on, Bertha's mind whirred. "Would you mind repeating that that?"

The congregation snickered. Her mother gasped.

The Vicar repeated everything and Bertha held onto hope. He'd identified the bride and groom by their full and proper names. If she agreed, perhaps it meant that she would be marrying the proper marquess after all. The vicar hadn't said, "Do you take this man?" he'd identified Leo by his full name.

"I will take Leopold, John Thaxton Grove, the fourth marquess of Hadlow." She said, clearly so that even the guests up the back could hear.

The Vicar turned to the doddery retainer, who looked as if he was in his cups, leaning forward with his eyes closed.

Her true loved elbowed the old man in the side and prompted him with, "I will."

The doddery old duffer woke up and blurted, "I will."

The rest of the proceedings were a total blur. Any time

Bertha tried to look towards Leo, he kept his eyes front. Not even a wink this time? What was he playing at?

The Vicar announced them marquess and Marchioness. The congregation sang a hymn from the book of common prayer.

While the congregation sang, the vicar directed Bertha, Braddon and Leo to a small antechamber, where they signed the register. Bertha's hand shook so much she struggled, but in the end, she had no choice. There was her signature, underneath the vicar's, in the church book for all eternity.

What a hideous mess!

She sat down and tried to capture her breath. The noise of a thousand buzzing flies filled her ears.

They returned to the estate, in the marquess's carriage. She and the doddery old retainer, and the marquess still pretending to be the butler.

"Leo I thought you were going to stop the wedding. To announce to all that you were the marquess and ... fix all of this mess?" She begged.

"And upset your mother? I couldn't possibly disappoint her with a scandalous wedding ceremony. And she got what she wanted, a coronet for her daughter."

It was too late to cry, but heat pricked her eyes anyway. "But you didn't get what you wanted, and neither did I."

"Oh ye of little faith," he said, and winked at her.

Merely a single wink during the ceremony would have reassured Bertha that everything was going to be all right. A wink in the carriage ride back to breakfast? Worthless!

CHAPTER 10

The wedding breakfast consisted of groaning tables of delicious food, but Bertha couldn't eat a bite.

The same affliction did not apply to the guests, who wished them all well, kissed the bride and shook the old groom's hand, then wished them a lifetime of happiness.

Bertha locked her face into a smile and committed herself to bearing through it. After all, in a few hours, it would be over. She might even get some peace and quiet. Even though she wasn't sure who she'd actually married today. Was it Leo, the real marquess, or the old man?

Her old husband drank deeply and had to be carried up to his room. Thank goodness. She would surely not be expected to lie with him. Nor would anyone expect he could do his duty.

Once the staff returned from carrying the old man away, the guests made their excuses to leave.

Leo, still playing at being a butler, helped move them out of the house with the promise their carriages were awaiting them outside.

Finally, Bertha bade her parents farewell. They were the last to leave.

She turned to find Leo chortling away to himself. He reached out and took her hand, then drew her in for an embrace.

"What are we going to do?" She asked.

"We could do this," he tilted her face up and planted a kiss on her lips. Warm and intoxicating. It sent sprigs of blossoms unfurling through her body. Oh, how her heart ached at the sweetness of it.

When Bertha pulled back, ending the dream kiss, she declared, "Mamma is going to find out eventually that I married a butler, not a marquess."

"No, my darling," He said as he took her hand. "We truly are wed."

Bertha wasn't sure she could cope with any more confusion. "But I'm married to him," she said, pointing in an upstairs direction.

Leo kissed her again and took her hand. "Come with me."

In a few minutes, they were in a smaller carriage heading back to the church. Or as Bertha called it, "her scene of deepest dismay". Her dearest love took her hand and walked her directly to the vestry and made her look upon the register.

"Think carefully, whose name did the vicar read out?"

"He read your full name out, and I was very clear about repeating your full name, if you recall correctly."

"Indeed. And, casting your mind back, who replied first?"

It had to be the wedding wine muddling her brain. "I thought Braddon said, "I will""

"Immediately before that, do you recall? I spoke first, making it look like I was prompting the old dear."

"Please don't raise my hopes like this, it is most unfair."

"But It's true, Bertha my darling. I was the one who replied first. And my darling, look upon the signatures in registry."

Bertha looked. Under the section for the bride, she saw her own nervous scrawl. But in the groom's section, she saw Leo's confident signature. He'd stepped in and signed as the groom, and the valet had signed as the witness!

"And so you see, my darling, we truly are wed."

She kissed him with all the love she had in her. Eventually she pulled away and asked, I still don't comprehend. Why did you go through with it? Why didn't you say who you were?"

"And give anyone a reason to stop it? Not on your life. Those Mammas out there will try any trick in the book to get me shackled to their daughters. This way, if they truly thought the old man was the real marquess, none of them were particularly upset that their daughter wasn't the one he'd chosen. If they'd known I was the marquess all along, I would have had them pulling all sorts of escapades to ensnare me."

"I see. That is rather clever. And I do feel that now I am wed, and others feel I have wed such an old man, I probably shan't have many visitors interrupting either. It is all rather ingenious."

"Thank you."

"However, there is a flaw. You have become wed, nonetheless. To me, apparently."

"Yes, I am, and It's going to be truly marvelous, because I do admire and love you so terribly."

Those noisy flies filled her ears again, and something else. Butterflies in her stomach. "Oh Leo, I do love you so. We are truly wed then?"

"We are indeed. Well, actually, we are not yet, in deed, if you get my meaning."

Heat spread over Bertha's neck and face, "Oh yes, the deed!"

"We should return home, my darling wife."

Bertha kissed Leo with all the love she could. "Careful, my darling husband, you're starting to sound sensible!"

If you enjoyed this sweet romance, then turn the page for the first chapter in another sweet Regency novella, *The Christmas Earl*.

MISS REMINGTON'S
STEELY RESOLVE

CHAPTER 1

LONDON, DECEMBER 1815

The young lady, Miss Waverley, fidgeted silently with her reticule as her mama, Mrs Waverley, of the Pembroke Square Waverleys, extolled her daughter's numerous virtues. "She sings charmingly, but only for private gatherings of friends and family, never in public. She eschews late evenings. She reads only the most appropriate materials, and never squints at the page. Needlework is where she truly excels. She will make a fine wife for a Viscount or Earl. I trust if we take a membership, the necessary introductions will take place at the next assembly?"

The widow, Mrs Lamb, poured the tea as she listened. From time to time she nodded, but said nothing in the negative. She also said nothing in the affirmative either, leaving Mrs Waverley to rush into the gap in conversation and keep talking about her wonderful, flawless daughter, as if the young woman was not at this moment sitting in the very same room.

Amelia Remington sat quietly near her aunt, Mrs Lamb. Needlework in hand, Amelia was there to be seen but not heard. It was an excellent circumstance, as it meant Amelia could eavesdrop with utter impunity. The discussion would never turn to her, and she would not be asked her opinion.

Not whilst the Waverley women were in attendance at least. Later, she and her aunt would speak, and Amelia would get out her book, flicking through the pages for the most suitable match for such an exemplary and quiet creature.

Did the young girl speak at all?

Amelia stitched a thread, then stored another morsel of information away from Mrs Waverley for future reference. Stitch and store, store and stitch.

"Naturally," Aunt Lamb said her first words in what might have been ten minutes. "It is a most convivial setting for match making, and far superior to any other. Our system has produced a great many happy matches. Our butler, Simmonds, handles the bookings, so please make your donation to the cause with him."

Aunt Lamb never directly took anybody's money. That would be unseemly.

"Yes," Lady Waverley agreed. "I shall send a messenger with the funds. Do you have the vouchers to dispense, so that we may plan which events to attend?"

Amelia nearly dropped a stitch at this morsel of information. Goodness, this Mama was getting directly to the point, wanting the vouchers before she departed, without parting with any money.

Amelia wound her thread about the needle, then pushed it through the fabric to make a French knot, all the time wondering whether Miss Waverley had much of a dowry to speak of.

Because a dowry was a topic that had definitely gone unmentioned during the entire meeting.

Aunt Lamb coughed into her hand and rang the bell for a maid. The maid came with a tray and cleared away the empty teacups and pot. This meeting was over.

"I do not carry the vouchers on my person," Aunt Lamb began, "as I'm sure you'll understand, that way I cannot be accused of playing favourites with any of the young ladies searching for husbands, nor with any of the many, *many* eligible and titled gentlemen who attend my functions. It is not a woman's lot to handle money, we are blessedly free from such things."

The stitches would not take, as Amelia furiously concentrated on her hooped fabric, praying she did not burst out laughing at the intricate way the women danced around the subject of paying for services. Amelia Remington had no doubt in her mind that if Aunt Lamb gave the Waverleys the vouchers now, payment would never come.

Simmonds, their butler, had proven his worth time and again, being the perfect foil for the money-handling side of the business. He had developed an art to opening the ledger and entering someone's name whilst they were dithering about payment. Once their name was inked onto the page, they rarely backed out of the deal, lest someone else see their name crossed out in that very legible ledger.

No matter what their situation, Amelia had instructed Simmonds, if the customer didn't pay, they didn't get the vouchers. Bless the man, he'd obeyed them to the very letter. After all, it was in his best interests this endeavor maintained its success, and its discretion, and Amelia's role in the operation. Yes, requiring money ahead of services was a tad mercenary, but then, so was the marriage market.

Fifteen minutes later, the Waverleys senior and junior had departed Lamb House, Amelia and Aunt Lamb none the wiser for knowing if they'd paid or not. They could check the ledger and remaining vouchers, but they were confident Simmonds had handled it.

Aunt Lamb rang the bell for the maid, who entered before the pealing had fully ended.

"More tea for my niece, and a brandy for me."

The maid bobbed a curtsey and set to it.

"Shall I ask the terrible question that was not raised at all during the meeting with Miss Waverley?" Amelia asked.

"No need," Aunt Lamb took a seat by the window. "The girl has no dowry, of that I'm sure. Her only chance of securing a marriage is to compromise a peer of some kind. If that started happening at our assemblies, word would spread faster than typhus and we'd be in all sorts of strife."

"We'd be on the street," Amelia agreed.

"Worse than that," Aunt Lamb turned to her, "You'd have to marry!"

The women both laughed, and Amelia added a jovial, "Anything but *that*!"

The maid returned with the requested refreshments. Amelia abandoned her embroidery and accepted the tea. Aunt Lamb sipped her brandy and sighed noisily. It was only the two of them alone here, and they both giggled. Amelia moved to the escritoire and pulled open a drawer to extract several curled pages wrapped with a ribbon. She then took out the family's much-thumbed edition of Debrett's and flicked through it.

Aunt Lamb took another sip of her brandy and declared, "I'll bet you a new pretty blue ribbon for your bonnet there's no Waverley Baronetcy."

"You are correct, Aunt, there is no Baronet Waverley. I cannot even find the Pembroke branch of such a name."

"I knew it."

Amelia closed the book that was so essential to their business. "It is a shame, however, as that means we are still lopsided for the next assembly. We have four and twenty gentlemen and only twenty ladies."

Aunt Lamb smacked her lips after another sip of brandy. "You could always join in."

With a shake of her head, Amelia said, "That brandy has loosened your tongue, Aunt. Nothing in the world could make me participate in an assembly, for I shall never marry."

"You may have to, to even out the numbers."

"Not if I can help it."

"Oh, come now, you will marry eventually, will you not?"

"I will not. I will not have my husband pass on a hideous disease from the continent to hasten my death, let alone die in childbed in a desperate attempt to give him an heir."

Aunt Lamb put her brandy down on her side table and stood up, arms wide for an embrace. "My darling girl, I still grieve for your mother, as you must as well. Married men can easily die as well."

The reminder of her aunt's widowed status weighed heavily with Amelia. Aunt Lamb had not married until the age of twenty-three, and had not been married long when her husband had been called away to the Navy. When the news of his gallant death had finally reached her in London, she'd fetched an Atlas to find the Adriatic Sea to discern her husband's final resting place. No, it wasn't somewhere she could easily visit to lay flowers on his watery grave. It was several months' journey away. It may as well be on the other side of the globe. That had been four years ago, and Aunt Lamb had declared she would not wed again. Not that she stopped hoping for Amelia.

Amelia took their curled membership papers and spread them out onto the floor, playing matchmaker with the names. The key was to match people's personalities as much as their purses. And their aspirations. Also, their comparative heights as well. Thin, wispy lords could be matched with anyone, really, and their constitutions would probably improve after marriage. But slim young women who could blow away in a gust of wind would not make it to their first anniversary with a brute. In the wrong hands, matchmaking could be a bloody business, but Amelia was determined to make sure nobody suffered.

Moving the papers about, she placed them at an imaginary supper table. Where she seated people could have enormous ramifications for the rest of their lives. The responsibility weighed heavily. The door to their room opened.

What? They weren't expecting anyone else. Aunt Lamb sat up straight. Simmonds bowed and announced their new visitor.

"Mrs Lamb, Miss Remington, the Ardalith of Caernarfonshire."

"The what?" Aunt Lamb said.

The man in question took off his hat and made a generous bow. "The Ardalith of Caernarfonshire, at your service."

Imaginary harps strummed in Amelia's ears as she looked upon the most intriguing face. He looked delightfully unkempt, as one who'd come from a long journey could. On him it added a layer of vitality rather than fatigue. Sparkling brown eyes under well-cut eyebrows looked down on her. Perhaps it was the angle - she so low on the floor and he standing at full height, but his legs appeared exceedingly long. Oh goodness, she was staring! Heat rose up her neck and covered her face.

"Where's Carnation-shur?" Aunt Lamb demanded.

Oh dear, Amelia wondered if the brandy had addled Aunt's senses. He could be a new subscriber. Judging by his clothes of the latest mode, he had funds. He would be a useful advertisement for more debutantes to attend their season of soirées.

With a hint of burr in his accent, he said, "Caernarfonshire is in The Lord's own country, northern Wales. Ardalith is Welsh for Marquess."

Quickly, Amelia gathered up the papers and letters from the floor and bundled them together. She stood up and slotted them onto the nearest shelf, before she turned and extended her hand in greeting.

Aunt Lamb made introductions. "My Lord, this is my niece, Miss Amelia Remington."

"A pleasure to make your acquaintance, My Lord," she said.

He took her hand and bowed neatly over it, then kissed the air above her skin. Despite the lack of contact, heat stole over her hand and floated up her arm. Any moment now she'd swoon, like the silly debutantes who barely made a peep during Aunt Lamb's interviews.

And yet he very much was worth swooning over.

As the man in swooning-contention rose back to full

height, he then nodded courteously to Aunt Lamb. "I have it on good authority that you are the society matron who may introduce me to my future bride?"

"I am," Aunt Lamb fussed a little with her skirts. Amelia smiled to herself at her aunt's momentary discomfort. Perhaps she too was overwhelmed by the striking specimen of manhood standing in their receiving room, his chestnut hair thick and windswept. "We were not expecting any further appointments this afternoon."

He looked surprised. "I sent a messenger ahead with a letter, but he must have been waylaid."

Amelia had a basket of correspondence she had not yet read through. The Ardalith's message could be amongst those. Alas, with the applications being what they were, their assemblies were already oversubscribed for gentlemen. They needed more young ladies. Unfortunately for the recently interviewed Miss Waverley, Amelia doubted her family would purchase vouchers in time.

Aunt Lamb recited her often repeated rules: "Our interviewing hours are strictly between two and four of an afternoon. Please make a booking with the butler on your way out, and we shall see you at our next available appointment."

"Ah yes, well," the Ardalith borrowed some time and ran his hand through his curls, "That's rather excellent. As it's not yet four, why don't we conduct the interview right now in a minute?"

What a strange way of speaking.

Amelia had to intervene. "Good things come to those who wait. We, I mean, Aunt Lamb, will need to read your letter first, then search through her files to ascertain your best likelihood for a match, and then conduct an interview."

"Well yes, very well," he said, "But to be honest, I'm in a rush." He gifted her with a beatific smile of neat creamy teeth. "I need to sail on the tide next week, before the weather turns really nasty, and I'll take my new bride home with me."

Aunt Lamb coughed softly into her handkerchief.

Concern filled his face, "I can pay, if that's what you're worried about. The Lamb matchmaking reputation has spread far and wide, that's why I'm here. But I cannot dilly dally in London. I have work to do before the bad weather sets in."

It was already winter. Amelia wondered how bad the weather might be in North Wales?

They called Simmonds the butler back in and asked him to get the bookings ledger. He returned a few moments later with the necessaries.

"Do we have any vacancies tomorrow?" Amelia asked.

The Marquess said, "You're an excellent assistant, your aunt must bless you on a daily basis."

"Oh yes," Aunt Lamb readily agreed. "Don't know what I'd do without her."

The butler looked upon the page, his eyes scrolling down, shaking his head left and right as he did so, giving every impression there were no vacancies in what must be a full timetable.

Aunt Lamb added, "It is a very busy time of year, as you'd understand. A great many of our gentlemen clients are keen to make a match before Christmas, but a hurried match can be a terrible thing. A woman enjoys the wooing."

The Marquess ran his hand through his hair again. Amelia's fingers itched to replace his.

He sounded as if he might apologise. "Under any other

circumstances, I'd agree with you. As I'm in a rush, I'm prepared to pay extra for a willing woman."

Now it was Amelia's turn to cough, in shock and ... she wasn't sure what the other thing was. A strange warmth unfurled somewhere inside.

Shock took precedence; they'd never had such a fast suitor approach them, and it quite spun her head. And as this was Aunt Lamb's business, at least on the surface, there was little Amelia could say.

Simmonds interrupted, "We have the Waverley appointment next Thursday, if they don't make it, this gentleman could take their place?"

Ah yes, the shy Miss Waverley. Even Amelia didn't think that would be fair on the poor girl to kick her off the books so soon. Especially as they had far too many men.

Aunt Lamb announced, "Good matches cannot be rushed."

Amelia simply had to say something, even though it would not normally be her place. "As you said, My Lord, Aunt Lamb's reputation has reached Wales, which means a great deal to us. But one poor match could permanently damage her reputation, and that simply would not do. Much less the shackled couple involved, who are destined to be miserable until the Lord calls them."

The man beamed with satisfaction. "Excellent point. And you'd know this, as I'm sure your aunt has you attached to a fine gentleman."

Shocked at how brazen he sounded, Amelia had to correct him. "I am not attached to any man, My Lord."

"Marvellous! Then this interview is concluded. I shall be back to collect you and your belongings in the morning."

Amelia was lost for words.

Aunt Lamb found hers. "Excuse me?"

"Miss Remington," The Marquess said, "She'll do me very well. I'll come back for her tomorrow. I'll treble the usual fee if you throw in a few servants."

* * *

What extraordinary luck to find a woman who could read! David beamed as he sauntered away from the Lamb residence and hailed a hackney to his lodgings near the docks. Miss Remington would make a most excellent wife. Mentally, he checked off her accomplishments as the cab rattled down the streets. Her golden hair gleamed with robust health. She looked well-nourished, and her pulse beat steadily as he'd held her hand. Definitely a sign of a good constitution. It was a technique he'd learned over the years checking horses and cattle. But it was the reading part that seriously impressed him. An excellent skill, and something that would be useful for helping him run his estates. Marvellous!

Although sailing around Britain was uncomfortable at times, it was a necessary evil of doing business around their sceptred isle. He preferred sailing to coach travel as he did not get seasick, and it was faster. A ship had no need to change horses along the way, and he could sleep in his cabin.

Sea voyages gave him the excuse not to read. He'd read nothing during his most recent sailing and had been free from those atrocious headaches for an entire week. Glory be!

His healthy euphoria must explain why he'd offered for Miss Remington so quickly. He was practically a giddy lad again, now that his headaches were gone.

When he reached the Inn, he paid John Coachman and headed inside for an ale. The taproom was crowded with men who looked suspiciously like sailing folk. Oh dear, they looked suspiciously like the crew of *Lady Rebecca*, which would be sailing within a few days.

"Ahh, Cennar-fon-shrrr," a man yelled.

Yes, definitely the same crew.

David greeted him with a wary smile.

The crewman nodded and said, "The boat's sprung a leak. We'll be a few weeks yet. We can unpack your boxes if you want to go home by road instead."

Bother! That meant he'd have to consult listings and read through tables of departure times and destinations. He could feel a headache coming on at the thought of it.

"An ale please, Landlord!" He said to the man behind the bar.

He would think about this tomorrow. As much as reading bothered him, reading by daylight was a far better option than reading by a flickering candle.

EPISTLE TO MISS BLOUNT

ON HER LEAVING THE TOWN,
AFTER THE CORONATION

As some fond virgin, whom her mother's care
    Drags from the town to wholesome country air,
    Just when she learns to roll a melting eye,
    And hear a spark, yet think no danger nigh;
    From the dear man unwillingly she must sever,
    Yet takes one kiss before she parts for ever:
    Thus from the world fair Zephalinda flew,
    Saw others happy, and with sighs withdrew;
    Not that their pleasures caused her discontent,
    She sighed not that They stayed, but that She went.
    She went, to plain-work, and to purling brooks,
    Old-fashioned halls, dull aunts, and croaking rooks,
    She went from Opera, park, assembly, play,
    To morning walks, and prayers three hours a day;
    To pass her time 'twixt reading and Bohea,
    To muse, and spill her solitary tea,
    Or o'er cold coffee trifle with the spoon,
    Count the slow clock, and dine exact at noon;
    Divert her eyes with pictures in the fire,

Hum half a tune, tell stories to the squire;
Up to her godly garret after seven,
There starve and pray, for that's the way to heaven.
Some Squire, perhaps, you take a delight to rack;
Whose game is Whisk, whose treat a toast in sack,
Who visits with a gun, presents you birds,
Then gives a smacking buss, and cries – No words!
Or with his hound comes hollowing from the stable,
Makes love with nods, and knees beneath a table;
Whose laughs are hearty, tho' his jests are coarse,
And loves you best of all things – but his horse.
In some fair evening, on your elbow laid,
Your dream of triumphs in the rural shade;
In pensive thought recall the fancied scene,
See Coronations rise on every green;
Before you pass th' imaginary sights
Of Lords, and Earls, and Dukes, and gartered Knights;
While the spread fan o'ershades your closing eyes;
Then give one flirt, and all the vision flies.
Thus vanish scepters, coronets, and balls,
And leave you in lone woods, or empty walls.
So when your slave, at some dear, idle time,
(Not plagued with headaches, or the want of rhyme)
Stands in the streets, abstracted from the crew,
And while he seems to study, thinks of you:
Just when his fancy points your sprightly eyes,
Or sees the blush of soft Parthenia rise,
Gay pats my shoulder, and you vanish quite;
Streets, chairs, and coxcombs rush upon my sight;
Vexed to be still in town, I knit my brow,

Look sour, and hum a tune – as you may now.

Alexander Pope, 1711

THE BOOKSHOP BELLES

NOVELS CO-WRITTEN
WITH CATHERINE BILSON:

Estelle's Ardent Admirer

Marie's Merry Gentleman

Louise's Christmas Champion

Bernadette's Dashing Doctor

THE BOOKSHOP BELLES

In the bustling market town of Hatfield, the four Baxter sisters are doing their best to manage Baxter's Fine Books while their father is away on a book-buying expedition in France. Each sister has her own strengths and dreams, but keeping the bookshop afloat will require all their combined wit, determination, and courage.

From fiery debates to slow-burn romance, the sisters find themselves tangled in unexpected love stories that challenge their beliefs and test their hearts.

• **Estelle**, the practical eldest, clashes with a charming gentleman who upends her carefully ordered life.

• **Marie**, the steady and sensible sister, is stranded in a snowbound castle with a brooding earl and his mischievous sons.

• **Louise**, the no-nonsense protector of the family, finds herself drawn to a towering former soldier with secrets of his own.

• **Bernadette**, the compassionate healer, must learn to work with a dashing doctor whose modern methods challenge everything she holds dear.

Set against the backdrop of a cosy bookshop and a charming Regency town, *The Bookshop Belles* is a heartwarming series about love, family, and the courage it takes to follow your heart.

Perfect for fans of sweet historical romance, these witty, slow-burn love stories feature strong heroines, dashing heroes, and happy endings without on-page sexual content.

ABOUT EBONY OATEN

Ebony Oaten loves history, but doesn't like living through it.

She is especially glad she was not around during the Regency era, as she would most likely have died in infancy from asthma, or something hideous like diphtheria. In the unlikely event that she'd made it to adulthood, she would have probably been a scullery maid or a lowly servant, as she 'talked too much and didn't pay attention' because ADHD diagnoses hadn't been invented.

Grab a free, sweet Regency romance novella and join her reading community here.

Or, if you like spicier reads, grab a free, steamy Regency romance novella and join her reading community here.

(You can grab both, and she'll delete email double-ups, it's all good.)

You'll find her website, full of Regency romance catnip, at www.ebonyoaten.com